Journey to Openworld

Wim Coleman and Pat Perrin
Illustrated by Jeremy Tugeau

Rigby

Contents

1

Sailing on the *Leif*

Outside the spacecraft's viewing port, nothing seemed to move. The stars were bright and beautiful, but there was no atmosphere to make them twinkle. Even the lightsail that rose from the ship and spread across space appeared frozen and still. The web of fine wires and computer chips looked like a giant fishing net.

Of course, Susannah knew that they were actually hurtling through space faster than human beings had ever traveled before. The *Leif* had been powered by a laser beam which originated on a platform at the outer reaches of Earth's solar system. For several years now, this laser beam had pushed against the huge lightsail, propelling the spacecraft at a speed close to that of light. And at last the journey was almost over.

Susannah leaned her forehead against the glass. She could feel the slight vibration of the ship's life-support system and hear its faint hum. Other than that, the *Leif* was silent.

Susannah sighed. She was on the greatest mission of exploration in human history. But all she really wanted to do was go home. Home to Earth.

A hand on her shoulder startled Susannah. "What do you think?" a soft voice asked.

Susannah turned to look at her mother. Laura Clearwater's eyes sparkled with excitement. Susannah knew that as far as her mother was concerned, this was the adventure of a lifetime. And it probably will be, thought Susannah. A lifetime for both of us.

However, she didn't express her thoughts. Instead she shrugged and said, "That I'll be glad to get there at last, I suppose."

"We all will, Susannah," said a loud, cheerful voice. The speaker was Angie Mays, who had just made her way to the viewing port. Angie, along with her husband, Wally, was another member of the expedition. Like all the adults on this mission, Angie and Wally were scientists with talents in many areas. Both were experienced space pilots. Angie was also a noted chemist, and Wally an electronics expert.

Susannah mentally reviewed the list of her fellow travelers. There was Alistair Oldham, the leader of this intergalactic exploratory mission. "Doc," as he was known, was in his mid-sixties. He was often called "a 22nd-century Ben Franklin" because of his wide-ranging interests. The former astronaut was also an inventor and a physicist.

Then there was Susannah's mother, a botanist and

agronomist who specialized in studying the potential for growing crops on other planets.

The last adult member of the expedition was Nelson Barrow, a physician and an amateur geologist.

Rounding out the group were its two youngest members: Susannah and Brent Oldham, Doc's grandson. Brent had gone to live with his grandfather at the age of seven, after his astronaut parents had been killed in a space accident. The same accident that had claimed the life of Susannah's father.

Five years ago, thought Susannah. Though it really was much longer than that now, she knew. She had been eleven years old when she boarded the *Leif.* Brent had been twelve. They had been traveling through space for years now. So, back on Earth, they would both be teenagers.

However, they weren't. Susannah and Brent were actually only a few months older than they had been when they started the mission. The same thing was true for the adults. They had all spent most of the journey in a state of suspended animation, safely strapped into travel pods. The *Leif* had hurtled though space without a pilot's hand at the controls. Computers had done the job.

A few hours ago, the computers had awakened them. Now Wally was at the controls, guiding the spacecraft to its first destination.

Suddenly a hearty voice boomed out, "Look at this, everyone!"

Susannah reached out to grab a handhold and make

her way toward Doc. He, Brent, and Nelson were staring out a second viewing port on the other side of the *Leif*. Her hand slipped and she bounced first against the side of the ship, and then into Nelson.

"Hey, watch it," said Nelson with a touch of impatience. "There's no gravity in here, remember?"

"Sorry," muttered Susannah as she clutched at another handhold. I *would* bump into him, she thought. Nelson Barrow wasn't her favorite adult. He was somewhat standoffish and prickly. Irritating him seemed to be a chronic problem for Susannah. So she tended to avoid him as much as was possible in the close environment.

Steadying herself, she slowly edged toward Doc and Brent. The older man turned to greet her, a wide smile peeking out from beneath his bushy gray mustache. Susannah couldn't help but smile back. Doc's enthusiasm was contagious.

"Look at this, Susannah!" he exclaimed, gesturing with one hand. "You, too, Laura and Angie. It's marvelous!" He moved aside so the others could see.

Susannah gasped in amazement. Where there had been nothing but tiny sparks of light and the blackness of space, a large whitish-yellow star could now be seen. It seemed to grow bigger by the second, as though it were speeding toward them. How unreal it looked among all the more distant, unchanging stars!

"Pele!" she exclaimed with awe.

"Our new sun!" Angie said in a rare whisper.

"The light of our new planet," Doc added with a smile. "Or at least, what *may* be our new planet."

New sun, new planet, thought Susannah. New to us, perhaps. But might it be old to somebody else—just like America was old to the Native Americans when the Europeans first arrived?

Though she was the child of scientists, Susannah's first love was ancient history. She read constantly, enthralled by stories of life before technology. So it was natural that now she thought of the daring explorers who had set out from Europe to cross the Atlantic Ocean. People like Columbus and Magellan and the Vikings. In fact, this spaceship had been named *Leif* after Leif Ericsson, a Viking explorer.

But Susannah's reading made her aware of more than the deeds of long-ago explorers. It also told her of the people whose lives were completely changed by their European visitors. The natives who were killed by newcomers who wanted their land. The others who lost their lives to diseases brought from a more "civilized" world.

And so a nagging thought had been bothering Susannah since she had first heard about this mission. Was history about to repeat itself?

However, the excitement of the moment made her forget her misgivings. The *Leif* had reached another solar system. And the people aboard were the first to have ever traveled so far.

"How long will it be before we land?" she asked. "Are we almost there?"

"You sound like a little kid," Angie replied.

"I just want to know," protested Susannah.

"We all do," her mother added.

"An hour or so, I think," said Doc. "Wally will have a better idea."

The pilot responded from his position in front of the control panels. "According to the computer, not even that long, Doc. So everybody better take a seat and get strapped in."

The others obeyed at once, knowing that soon the spacecraft would encounter Openworld's gravitational pull. And within minutes, an alarm went off, telling them that it had.

"This is it!" called Wally. "Next stop—Openworld!"

Susannah rested her head against the seat back, sensing her own weight for the first time since leaving the space station where the mission had begun.

Beside her, Brent spoke excitedly. "The sail caught the light from Pele," he said. "That gives Wally the power to slow the ship and steer us into Openworld's orbit. And then to land on the planet's surface."

Susannah didn't respond. She knew all of this. Just like she knew that if Pele's light hadn't hit the sail, as planned, the *Leif* would have hurtled right on by Openworld.

Sailing on the *Leif*

Disconnected from the laser beam, the spacecraft depended on an external source to provide it with power. Otherwise, the *Leif* would simply coast through space forever—or until it collided with something else. She shook her head, trying to clear it of unpleasant thoughts.

Silence fell over the group as they waited for the long journey to end. The only sounds to be heard were the hum of the life-support system and a few low grunts from Wally. Then the pilot called out, "OK, folks, here goes. We're exiting the orbit and heading for the surface."

There was a roar of rockets. Then the ship suddenly shuddered and shook violently. A knot of fear settled in Susannah's chest.

"What's happening?" Angie cried in alarm.

"I'm not sure," Wally replied, examining the computer screens. "I think the sails are getting too much light. We're slowing down too fast!"

"Well, do something!" Nelson shouted.

"Everyone calm down," ordered Doc in a measured voice. "Let Wally do his job."

There was another jolt. The walls of the *Leif* creaked and groaned. Susannah felt a sickening sensation in her midsection, as if she were in a falling elevator.

She squeezed her eyes shut. She was somewhat comforted by her mother's hand, which had reached out to take hers.

Susannah felt heavier and heavier. It was almost impossible to keep her eyes open. What if Wally was having the same problem? What if he passed out? And even if he didn't, would the ship survive long enough to reach Openworld?

A vision of the *Leif* hurtling toward the planet below filled her mind. If we do make it, Susannah wondered, will anyone be watching as our sail appears in the sky? She'd been told many times that there were no signs of life on this planet. Still, she couldn't convince herself of that. Not completely.

Her mind raced on. Will anyone be there to meet us? Will they be afraid? Will they be angry?

For a moment, Susannah had an image of long-ago people staring with amazement at the white sails of a strange ship. Other thoughts came to her as she drifted deeper and deeper into unconsciousness. Stories her mother had told her . . . memories of how this mission had come to be . . .

Past and Present

Pele and its planets had been discovered before Susannah had been born. They were first spotted by a giant space telescope that orbited at the outer edge of Earth's solar system. Most planets that had been discovered in other solar systems were large and gassy. No one could possibly live on them. But the planets closest to Pele looked small and solid, like Earth.

Scientists had been excited. Could there be life on these planets? Or were they places that could potentially support human life? A small unmanned probe had been sent to take a closer look.

Although Pele was one of the closest stars to Earth, it was still light-years away. So it took the probe years to reach Pele's planetary system. And then it took more years for the probe's radio signals to return to Earth. But the information it sent back was worth the wait.

As it sped past the second planet from that distant sun, the probe reported an atmosphere that contained oxygen. The planet even appeared to have some kind of plant life, though there was no sign of other living creatures. It looked so promising—so open to human development—that scientists named it Openworld.

The probe had gone on to other planets in Pele's system—in fact, it was still on its journey. Still sending data back to Earth.

At the time, Doc had been the head of a team of scientists who were working on a new type of spacecraft. Susannah's father had been one of these scientists.

Doc's experimental spacecraft was based on a recent discovery—a new type of laser. One that was strong enough to power a spacecraft tremendous distances at a speed close to that of light. Coupled with a lightsail, this laser was capable of transporting humans farther and faster than ever before.

A new solar system—and a new technology. At once, Doc decided that he would use his own money to fund a private mission to explore Openworld and other planets of Pele's solar system. And beyond that, to colonize the planet that showed the most promise.

Susannah's parents had been among the first to support Doc's idea. And to sign on as members of the mission.

Susannah didn't remember any of this herself. She had been too small to pay much attention. She did remember the excitement that had seemed to surround her parents, though. The conversations they had had about the great discoveries to be made. And about the benefits that Doc's mission could have for those on Earth.

And then, on a routine space flight, Susannah's father and both of Brent's parents had lost their lives.

Susannah and her mother had headed home—back to New Mexico. Laura Clearwater had gone on with her work. Susannah had gone back to being a regular kid.

And then, "Susannah, we need to talk," Laura had said one day.

"About what?"

"I heard from Doc yesterday."

"Oh," said Susannah, "is he coming to visit soon, Mom?" Doc and his grandson came to see the Clearwaters often.

"No. He wants us to go to see him."

"Where?"

"He's working on a space station right now," said Laura.

"Oh." Susannah's mind had raced—she wasn't sure if this sounded interesting or disturbing.

"Susannah, everything is almost ready for Doc's mission to Pele's solar system," said Laura. "And . . ."

"And what, Mom?" asked Susannah when her mother hesitated.

"And he's still looking for someone with my skills. He's asked me to consider joining him again. Asked us, I should say."

At first Susannah hadn't been able to respond. She knew what this meant. Doc's mission was no jaunt into space with a triumphant return in a few years. No—it was for much longer than that. Long enough to see if there was a habitable planet in the new solar system. For all practical purposes, it was *forever.*

"Susannah, this is an opportunity that we may never have again. To be the first to see new planets."

"But, Mom . . ."

"Will you think about it, sweetheart? I want you to be all right with going. There is no way I'm going to drag you away against your will."

"I'll think about it, Mom," said Susannah slowly. She looked up at her mother's excited face. "This is something Dad really wanted to do, isn't it?"

"Yes, but that's not the only reason *I* want to, Susannah. Doc's mission is to find places where human beings can live. You know how important that is. Eventually Earth is not going to have enough resources to support its population. Someone has to be working on solutions to that problem now."

Susannah had nodded. And the next day she had made her decision. She wouldn't stand in her mother's way. They were going to be space colonists . . .

A familiar voice, singing the words of a familiar song, broke into Susannah's uneasy dreams.

"Big old sloth, with great big toes,
Hanging upside-down in a chicle tree—
How you slumber, how you doze!
Won't you open your eyes for me?"

Susannah felt a hand on her forehead. She groaned

softly, not ready to get up. Was it morning already?

Then she heard a voice that definitely was not her mother's. "Are you going to come to, or what?"

Susannah's eyes snapped open. She wasn't in her bunk on the space station, where she had lived for the months before the mission actually started. She was strapped into a seat on the *Leif.* Her mother and Brent were staring down at her. Both wore slightly worried looks.

Suddenly things began to come back. Susannah hazily remembered the *Leif* creaking and shaking.

"Is everything all right?" she asked. "What happened?"

"Everything's fine," Mom said. "I was a little worried about you, that's all. You kind of passed out on us there."

Susannah's cheeks grew warm from embarrassment. "Some great explorer I am," she muttered as she started to get to her feet. She still felt a bit dizzy. And it wasn't easy to move. She wasn't weightless anymore.

"Are we on Openworld?" she asked.

"Go and see for yourself," Mom replied.

Just walking to the ship's open hatchway left Susannah gasping. "The air!" she gasped. "It's hard to breathe!"

"It's thin because there's less gravity here than on Earth," Brent explained. "It's all right, though. The air has a lot more oxygen than Earth's, so it's OK that it's thinner."

"Breathe slowly," Mom added. "You'll get used to it."

Susannah breathed in long and deeply, then breathed out ever so slowly. Mom was right. She felt better.

Then she noticed that sunlight was pouring into the *Leif*. Pele's light! she realized. She stood in the doorway, her heart pounding with excitement.

She was facing Pele, which appeared smaller than Earth's sun, but also whiter and brighter. It was actually somewhat larger and farther away, she knew. Susannah had to shield her eyes with one hand to get a better view. She studied the daytime sky—blue, but darker than Earth's sky. In the distance, a few pink clouds swirled above a ridge of low hills.

Her first impression was that this whole world was blue—a hundred different shades of blue. In some places, rocks sparkled in the sunlight like diamonds. It was as if Earth's oceans had frozen and become land.

"Why is everything so blue?" she asked.

Brent answered. "It's because most of the rocks are blue. So, of course, the soil is, too."

"And there are clear stones that reflect the blue colors," added Laura. "Nelson says they seem to be similar to quartz."

They stood there for some time, staring out at the landscape. Gradually the blue was less overwhelming to Susannah. Now she could see that the colors ranged all the way into purples, with spots of pink and orange here and there. The view wasn't actually *all* blue, as it had seemed at first.

She could see a pale, round moon rising in the sky,

smaller than Earth's moon. She knew that she would eventually see two more moons, because Openworld had three.

"Here we are," she murmured with wonder, "in a brand new world!"

3

Moons Over Openworld

As soon as the word "new" was out of Susannah's mouth, she knew what Brent would say.

He didn't disappoint her. "Actually, it's a very old planet," he said in his most matter-of-fact tone. "Much older than Earth."

Susannah found herself studying Brent as he spoke. Her friend was about her height, but much more muscular. His wiry, dark hair was cut short. The vision unit he wore hid his eyes and reflected the blueness of the planet. Brent had been born blind. However, he could "see" thanks to the vision unit and a computer chip implanted in his brain. The chip sorted out the images recorded by the vision unit and sent them to his brain—much as the eye did in a sighted person. Most blind people used similar technology, but Brent could actually see better than if he were fully sighted. This was because his vision unit was experimental—one of his grandfather's many inventions.

"Brent, does all of this look different to you than it does to me?"

Brent shrugged. "Most likely. Gramps says my vision unit picks up a wider range of light than the human eye. So I suppose I can see more. For example, there's a yellowish glow hanging over some of those rocks. Can you see it?"

Susannah looked in the direction Brent indicated. All she saw were shades of blue. "No," she responded. "I can't see that at all. What do you think it is?"

"A kind of energy, I suspect. Even on Earth, some minerals store energy and give it off."

Susannah's mother broke in on their conversation. "OK, you two, enough discussion. I want to get down there. Are you ready to set foot on Openworld?" she asked her daughter.

Susannah nodded. She waited for Brent and her mother to climb down ahead of her. Then she followed. As she made her way down the ladder, she realized that Openworld's lower gravity would take some getting used to. It was nothing like being weightless, but she didn't feel completely steady on her feet.

Outside, Susannah turned around and gazed back up at the *Leif.* The ship now looked like a simple aircraft with stubby wings. The lightsail and part of the spaceship were still in orbit overhead. The main section of the ship had separated from the rest for the landing. Using smaller sails to catch Pele's light, it had worked its way down to the planet's surface.

Those small sails had burned completely away when the ship entered Openworld's atmosphere. The ship itself was scorched and dirty. A long trail of skid marks showed that it had landed at high speed, despite the parachute that slowed it down. It seemed like a miracle that they had gotten here safely.

Suddenly, Susannah heard a familiar voice.

"Welcome to Openworld, Susannah!"

Doc was walking toward them. The team leader sported a wide grin beneath his grizzled mustache.

"It's quite a sight, Doc," said Susannah.

"Yes—beautiful, isn't it?" asked the scientist. He looked around in satisfaction. "And we're here—all of us—safe and sound."

"Wish we could say the same for the *Leif*," added a sour voice. It was Nelson Barrow, who had come up behind Doc. The scientist was tall and thin, with long gray hair caught at the back of his neck in a ponytail.

"What do you mean?" asked Susannah. "What's wrong with the ship?"

"Nothing that can't be fixed," said Doc. "Nothing to worry about."

Susannah's mother put an arm around her daughter's shoulders. "The *Leif* got knocked around a bit, Susannah, that's all. Wally and Doc can fix it. It will just take some work."

"But what if we have to leave?" asked Nelson. "What if

we discover that Openworld isn't the right place for us?"

"I don't think that's going to be the case," replied Doc. "But even if it is, Nelson, the ship will be fixed. If we have to leave, we'll be able to."

"Good," said the scientist. "Because I have to tell you, Doc, this isn't exactly what I had been hoping for." He looked out over the blue landscape with thinly veiled disgust. "There's not a sign of anything geologically interesting out there."

"Well," said Doc mildly, "it's not your interest in geology that makes you a valuable member of our team, Nelson. We depend on you to keep us healthy."

"Besides, there *are* some odd crystals scattered around," said Laura. "They're not like anything I've ever seen before."

"I suppose," Nelson said. Then he shook his head and grinned. "Sorry for whining. Guess I'm just a little disappointed."

"Well, we have plenty to do," said Doc, "and staying busy will take the edge off any disappointment we might feel."

Under Doc's direction, they all set to work carrying supplies from the *Leif*. In a matter of hours, they had assembled a large prefabricated dome. This would serve as temporary living quarters and laboratory while the group investigated the planet. The frame of the dome had snapped together like a giant building toy. The covering was actually the *Leif's* parachute—which was designed to fit over the frame like a glove. Transparent sections of the parachute even functioned as windows. And, at one seam, the parachute zipped open to accept a full-size door.

A satellite dish now sat atop the laboratory section. It had already been used to beam news of the *Leif's* safe landing. Susannah knew that the message would take a long time to actually reach a listener on Earth. But when it did, everyone would be thinking about Openworld. And waiting for news about whether or not another group of colonists should set out for the planet. A larger group.

"Well, folks, that's it," announced Doc as he studied the structure with satisfaction. "Our first home on Openworld."

Susannah gazed at the domed building. Home, she thought. Would she ever truly feel at home again?

Then Doc indicated a mass of clouds that had gathered overhead. "It looks like we finished just in time," he said. "I think we're in for a rainstorm. According to the data the probe collected, it rains every afternoon here. Pele's heat builds up until there's a storm."

He had hardly finished speaking when the rain started to fall. They all quickly sought shelter inside the dome.

Susannah stood and gazed out of the dome's entryway. Big drops splashed down onto the blue soil and were instantly absorbed. The rain gradually increased until she could see nothing beyond the walls of the dome. Then, as quickly as it had started, the storm ended. A steamy mist rose from the blue landscape. Within half an hour, not even a puddle remained as a sign that it had rained.

Later, an hour or so before sunset, Susannah and Brent sat by themselves on a low hill near the domed building. Openworld revolved once every 20 hours or so. That meant that its days and nights were shorter than Earth's.

The whitish Pele grew somewhat more yellow in color as it crept toward the horizon. In the changing light, Susannah noticed patches of dull green here and there among the stones. From this distance, they looked like moss.

"Do you think those green spots are some kind of plants?" she asked.

"Gramps says they probably are," Brent replied. "Your mom will know when she gets a chance to study them."

"Other than that, I don't see much here," Susannah remarked. "Just a rocky blue planet."

"And one with no real seasons," Brent added. "That's because Openworld doesn't tilt on its axis like Earth does. So it's probably like this on this part of the planet pretty much all the time. Warm all day with a rainstorm in the afternoon. Kind of like the tropics on Earth."

"We're a long way from home, aren't we?" Susannah asked softly. She wasn't surprised when Brent didn't answer.

It was a lovely sunset, she had to admit. Low-lying clouds caught Pele's last rays in shades of pink and powdery gray. They reflected this light upward in streaks of yellow, white, and orange.

As she watched, Susannah felt a dull ache deep inside. How strange it was to know that she might never watch another spectacular Earth sunset.

The last curved white edge of Pele slipped behind a faraway ridge. The sky instantly grew darker. At that moment, Brent broke the deep silence. "Susannah, look!"

All three of Openworld's moons floated overhead in the starry sky. They were smaller than Earth's moon, but every bit as bright.

"Do they have names?" Susannah asked.

"Not that I know of," Brent replied.

"Well, we should name them, then."

"The adults will probably want to do that," Brent observed.

"They'll just give these lovely moons stuffy old names out of some mythology book," complained Susannah. "So let's name them right now. Names *we* think they should have."

"Maybe you're right," agreed Brent. Susannah was surprised. Usually Brent was just as scientific and stuffy as any adult—in fact, more so.

She pointed to a moon. "That one's got a face in it, sort of like our man in the moon."

"Only it has a big clown nose," said Brent.

"And a silly grin," Susannah said. "So let's call it Emmett."

"Emmett?" repeated Brent. "Where did that come from?"

"Emmett Kelly. He was a famous clown centuries ago," explained Susannah.

Brent laughed. "OK, Emmett it is."

"The one to Emmett's right is dark around the edges. And it has a white stripe down the middle."

"Like a skunk," Brent suggested.

"OK, that's it," said Susannah. "Skunk."

"And the last moon is greenish with what looks like a dark valley at the center," Brent remarked. "Like the eye of a cat. So let's call it that: Cat's Eye."

"I like it," said Susannah. They repeated the names several times, testing the sounds: Emmett, Skunk, and Cat's Eye.

Susannah smiled in the darkness. Somehow naming the moons made Openworld seem more homelike. More welcoming.

Then something else caught her eye. She pointed to a

bright silver disk overhead. "Is that a meteor?" It was smaller than any of the moons. And it was moving—a silver coin floating through space.

"It's the *Leif's* lightsail," Brent explained. "It's still circling Openworld. If and when it's ever time to leave this planet, we can rocket back into orbit and reconnect with the sail."

"Then on to another planet," sighed Susannah.

"You don't sound all that excited about it. How come?"

"I don't know," answered Susannah slowly. "Maybe because I'm not." She turned to look at Brent, who was only a shadowy outline beside her. "Did you really want to come on this mission?"

"Yes, of course," said Brent. "It's the most exciting thing ever."

"I suppose," said Susannah. "But I think I would have preferred to stay put on Earth."

"Not me," said Brent. "I want to find out about this planet—and about others that are nearby. We're the first, Susannah. The first!"

When Susannah didn't respond, Brent continued. "Besides, you don't know yet that you won't like it here. Wait until we get a real colony going. Someday we'll have buildings and roads and lots of people. You might even end up thinking this is the best place in the universe to live."

"Better than Earth?" asked Susannah, thinking of trees and lakes and mountains.

"Maybe."

The two friends fell silent again. As Susannah watched the lightsail float across the sky, she thought again about her earlier fears. She had worried whether someone on Openworld might see the *Leif's* sail and react with fear or anger. That their coming might bring unhappiness or tragedy to the planet.

But nobody is here, Susannah thought now. Nobody can see the lightsail, except us.

It was a lonely thought.

It was a lonely planet.

4

First Explorations

The next morning, Susannah woke up feeling like she hadn't slept. Part of it was the fact that Openworld's nights were shorter than Earth's. It seemed as if Pele had come blazing up over the horizon only a few hours after she had tumbled into her cot.

Another reason for Susannah's restless night had been the troubled thoughts that continued to fill her mind. No matter how hard she tried, she couldn't rid herself of the feeling that someone—or something—must have noticed *Leif's* great lightsail. That someone had been here, watching them land.

She swung her feet over the edge of the cot and sat up. Beside her, her mother still slept. A thin partition separated their sleeping area from other sections of the living quarters. There wasn't a lot of room to spare. But then, they didn't have much with them in the way of personal belongings.

Susannah had lived in small places before. Several months on a space station, for example. And there, she hadn't had the potential of an entire planet to explore. She felt a little shiver of excitement make its way up her spine. Maybe today she could see something of her new home.

Half an hour later, everyone was up. Susannah sat with the others, picking at her breakfast. The food was hardly appetizing. It came in plastic trays and tubes and was beige and tasteless. Susannah sighed.

"Cheer up," her mother said. "It won't always be like this. Remember, we brought lots of seeds with us. And as soon as I can do some soil studies, we'll plant some experimental crops. Before you know it, you'll be complaining about eating peas."

Susannah grinned. "A few weeks of this, and I promise I'll never gripe about a pea again," she said.

"It will be interesting to see what Earth plants grow well in Openworld's soil," Laura said. "And if any of the mossy plants that we've spotted here are edible."

She fell silent and Susannah knew she was thinking of her work. Laura's role was vital. If the colonists couldn't grow or find food on this planet, they couldn't stay.

But if they could, then this would be a real colony. They would build permanent homes—larger and more private than their temporary quarters.

Thinking about houses and real food made Susannah feel a little better. And when she found out what her task was that morning, she cheered up even more.

"I have a job for you, Susannah," said Doc. "Two jobs, actually. Angie volunteered herself—and you—for both of them. First, the two of you can look for a source of water nearby. We know there is plenty of water on the planet. After all, it rains every day. We suspect that there are pockets of water that collect underground. We just have to figure out how we can get to them. So that's your first task."

"What's the other?"

"While the two of you are looking for water, you can also do some measuring for our homestead."

"You mean surveying?" asked Susannah.

Doc laughed. "That's what I mean," he said. "Not the whole planet," he qualified. "Instruments attached to the orbiting lightsail are doing that. Just measure where we'll set up housing."

Susannah remembered that each group or family of colonists that arrived on Openworld would stake off a one-square mile space. These would be called "homesteads," just as the plots of land claimed by western settlers of the United States had been.

Susannah tried to picture a square mile. It didn't seem like that much space. But then, there weren't that many people here to fill it.

Doc added, "Where we've put the dome will mark what is roughly the middle of the eastern boundary of our homestead. So you should start measuring from here."

"Come on, Susannah," said Angie as she rose to her feet. "Let's get to work."

Susannah was relieved that she wouldn't have to spend the day in the crowded work dome. There was plenty to be done there, but she would rather be outside in the sunshine. She knew Angie felt the same way, which was probably why she had volunteered to supervise the surveying.

Outside the dome, they paused to collect their gear. "Here we go," said Angie. "Measuring equipment, marking pegs, communicators, tazers."

"Why do we need tazers?" asked Susannah. "I thought you said there was nothing much living here. Nothing that we need to protect ourselves from, at any rate."

"We don't know that for sure," said Angie. "And it wouldn't pay to go exploring a new planet unarmed. You do know how to use a tazer, don't you?"

Susannah frowned. "Of course I do," she said. Tazers were relatively simple devices. They emitted a ray that could stun a living creature. Their range wasn't that great—only about six feet. And the creature wouldn't stay unconscious for longer than an hour or so—less time than that if it were something large. Still, she didn't like the idea of stunning anyone—or anything.

Angie sensed her unease. "Stash it in your utility pouch, Susannah," she said. "I doubt that you'll be using it. But you're not leaving the dome without it."

Susannah nodded. She dropped the tazer into the pouch that was clipped to her orange coveralls. Then she strapped a two-way radio communicator to her wrist and picked up a handful of plastic marking pegs.

They started measuring in front of the dome, just beyond the *Leif*. Susannah's job was simple. She stood where Angie told her to. In one hand, she held what looked like a ping-pong paddle with a long handle that reached to the ground. A light on the device told her when she was holding it straight up and down.

Angie would move some distance away and aim a small hand-held measuring device at Susannah. It bounced a beam of laser light off the paddle. Then the device would register the exact distance between the two of them. Once that was done, Susannah was supposed to stick a few pegs in the crumbly ground and move on to the next designated spot.

After the first two measurements, Angie said, "OK, let's get a rover. We've got quite a ways to go and that will make it faster."

Susannah followed Angie toward the *Leif*. Two small vehicles waited there in the shade of the spacecraft. The rovers were similar in appearance to the small robotic vehicles that had been used in early Mars explorations over a century before. However, these were large enough to carry four adults. And they were equipped with everything from radar to an optional remote-control feature.

Angie got in the driver's seat and Susannah climbed in next to her. As they headed away from the dome, Angie said, "We'll stop at the last peg you put in the soil."

From that spot, they made several more measurements. Then they hopped in the rover and moved on. This time Angie said, "Obviously, water is a priority. And hopefully we'll find some sign of it before we get too far from the dome. So keep your eyes open."

Susannah nodded. Her eyes darted back and forth as Angie drove. She wasn't exactly sure what to look for. She didn't expect to see a lake or river, since the probe that had orbited Openworld had shown nothing of the sort. But she thought she might spot a place where the sparse plants grew more thickly. That could be a sign of under-ground water.

Susannah continued looking for evidence of water as the measuring continued. Studying her surroundings carefully, she noticed that the plants seemed to grow in greater variety now. She saw some of the mossy plants that grew just outside the dome. But she also saw something with plantlike features that had very oddly shaped leaves. These leaves grew in every shade of green imaginable—all on the same plant. Except some of the leaves weren't green, but clear, almost like crystal. The plants grew on rocks as well as on the soil. She also saw plants that resembled ferns. These sprouted right on top of some rocks.

They can't have much in the way of roots, Susannah thought idly. Still, they looked healthy. She would have to tell her mother about them. Laura would want to collect samples and run tests to see if any of these plants could be eaten.

Before long, Angie and Susannah had measured their way about a quarter of a mile from the dome. Susannah observed another change. The plants were still the same in appearance, but now some of them seemed to grow in clumps. They looked almost like pictures Susannah had seen of medieval herb gardens that had been laid out in intricate patterns.

Fernlike plants circled boulders. Others fit into spaces surrounded by small rocks. And there was one patch of mossy plants that grew in the shape of a perfect triangle.

Almost like someone planted them that way, Susannah thought. Of course, the idea was silly. There wasn't anyone to plant them, after all. Still, she couldn't help wondering—how had the plants arranged themselves in such interesting ways?

By now Angie and Susannah had worked their way around to the back side of the dome. Only the top of the building was now in sight. The rest was hidden by a slight hill that rose behind it.

Following Angie's latest instructions, Susannah began to walk slightly uphill. Suddenly she tripped. The measuring device fell from her hand, clattering noisily against the rocks.

"Watch it, Susannah!" Angie shouted. "We don't want that to get broken."

"I couldn't help it," she protested, thinking that Angie

didn't seem to care if *she* got broken. "There's a big pot-hole here."

Susannah picked up the device and dusted off her coveralls. Then she looked ahead of her, up the hill. "Actually, there are a lot of potholes, Angie. Some really big ones."

Angie started to move closer. "Hmmm," she said, "those look like sinkholes."

"Sinkholes?" echoed Susannah. "You mean like the things that have swallowed cars and houses in Florida?"

"Yes. And that means there might be an underground river or lake in this area," Angie said. "So let's—"

Angie's suggestion was cut off by a surprised screech from Susannah. With a terrible crunching sound, the ground had dropped beneath her. She fell on her back and began sliding forward, feet first, toward a hole that grew wider by the second.

5

Something's Out There!

Susannah slid faster—and headed right into the hole. Her fingers grasped desperately at the ground, but there was nothing to grab hold of.

Suddenly a hand clasped hers, jerking her to a halt. For a moment, there was no sound except that of small rocks skittering toward the hole. And of the splash they made shortly after tumbling into it. Then Angie said in a calm voice, "Just stay still, Susannah. Don't move until I tell you to."

The hand tightened its grip, then began to pull Susannah away from the hole. "OK, kiddo, push along with your feet if you can," Angie instructed.

Susannah did so. To her relief, she began to move slowly away from the gaping hole. And, in a matter of minutes, she was lying on solid ground again.

"Whew!" said Angie, plopping down next to Susannah. "That was close."

Susannah got to her feet carefully, worried that the

ground might give way again. Where she had been walking earlier was now a large hole, at least four feet across.

"Well, Susannah, I think you found our water supply," said Angie.

"I think I almost ended up *swimming* in our water supply," corrected Susannah in a somewhat shaky voice. "Do you think we should get close enough to see how far down the water is?"

"I think maybe someone had better get the area around the hole shored up first," said Angie. "We can investigate when it's safer. And from now on, we test every footstep when we're in an unexplored region."

She looked at Susannah. "Are you game to keep surveying? We've still got a lot to do. But at least now we know there's water not far from the dome."

Susannah gazed once more at the sinkhole that had almost swallowed her. "Yeah," she said, "let's finish the job."

Angie clapped her on the back. "Good! I knew I could count on you."

As Angie turned away from the hole, Susannah gazed back at it. She couldn't help thinking about how terrified she had been. Then she blinked. Something was at the far side of the hole. Something that moved.

"What . . . ?" she murmured. She started toward the movement, then remembered the gaping hole and stopped. She blinked again. Yes, there was definitely something there. A gray blob. A gray blob that appeared to be alive.

"Angie, stop!" hissed Susannah in a low voice.

"Huh?" replied Angie. "Why, what's the matter?"

"There's something out there, Angie. I think it's alive."

As Angie hurried back to Susannah's side, the blob quivered. Then it disappeared over the horizon.

"It's gone!" she cried. "Did you see it?"

"I didn't see a thing, Susannah," said Angie. She gazed out at the rocky ridge that extended beyond the sinkhole. "There's nothing there, kiddo."

"I saw something!" insisted Susannah.

"Hey, you just had a really frightening experience. I'm not surprised you're seeing things. Now, do you want to finish up the surveying, or should we just get you back to the dome?"

"I want to finish," muttered Susannah. But I *did* see something, she thought. At least, I'm pretty sure I did.

Sighing, Susannah followed Angie away from the sinkhole. She noted that the older woman walked gingerly, testing every footstep. Susannah was careful to follow the path that Angie made. One near miss was enough for the day.

Two hours later, they were back at the dome, reporting on their surveying—and on their discovery of water nearby.

"From the splashes I heard, it's not that far down to the water," Susannah said.

"That's good," Doc responded. "Even with the rain we get, it will be essential to have plenty of water easily available."

"But is it safe to drink?" asked Brent.

"I'll do some tests today," Laura promised. "If the water's not drinkable as it is, we have methods of filtering and purifying it."

"There's one thing that worries me, Doc," Susannah said slowly. "Is it going to be OK to build near the water hole? I saw a lot of places near that sinkhole that looked like they could be pretty unsafe."

"That's definitely a consideration, Susannah," Doc replied. "For now, we'll concentrate on building east of the area where you found the water. The ground seems stable here. And there's plenty of room for now." He looked at the others. "So use the markings Angie and Susannah have made as a guide. Don't go wandering off where there are any signs of sinkholes. And don't go anywhere alone. Think of what might have happened if Angie hadn't been with Susannah."

They all nodded their agreement. It was all too easy to imagine what might have happened.

And Susannah had even more reason for not wanting to wander off. What if there was some strange creature out there? She thought about mentioning what she had seen. What she *thought* she had seen. But everyone would probably react as Angie had. She decided not to say anything. Maybe it had only been her imagination.

A week later, signs of progress were easy to spot. A rough platform surrounded the sinkhole. It was made from plastic lumber that had been part of the *Leif's* cargo. There was nothing high-tech about the space colonists' water-gathering methods. An old-fashioned pulley system lowered a container into the pool of clear water. Old-fashioned muscle power helped to bring it back up.

Laura had tested the water and pronounced it safe. Still, as a precaution, they decided to add purification tablets to the water they drank.

Susannah had been busy helping her mother sow some

test seeds in the blue soil of Openworld. Some had been planted in a small plot close to the dome. But most were growing in flats inside the laboratory section. Laura was experimenting with a variety of grain and vegetable crops that grew in different regions on Earth. How well these plants did would determine what the colonists would grow as actual crops here on Openworld. If things went well, the settlers could eventually feed themselves.

"Look at this," Laura said to her daughter as they examined the flats. Some seeds were already beginning to sprout, sending tiny green shoots up through the blue soil.

"Things seem to grow faster here than on Earth," she continued.

"Why do you think that is?" asked Susannah.

"I'm not sure yet. There seem to be substances in the soil that we don't have on Earth. That could be it. Or it could be the quality of Pele's light. Or something in the water. Or a combination of any of those factors. Time and testing will tell."

"What about those tiny wormy things we found?" asked Susannah. She remembered the first time her mother had dug beneath the blue surface. The soil had been dry and crumbly. And full of tiny brown wormlike creatures that quickly wriggled their way deeper into the soil.

"They could be a factor, too," admitted Laura. "I'm sure they break up the soil, just like worms do on Earth. However, I was careful not to bring any of them in with the dirt we put in these flats."

Susannah upended the water container she was using. "That's it for water," she said. "I should get some more."

"Do you want me to help? You know Doc doesn't want anyone going off alone."

"No, you stay here and work. I'll see if Brent wants to come along," Susannah said. "We'll take a rover. That way we can bring back a bunch of containers."

"Fine," said Laura absentmindedly. She made a few notes on a chart, hardly noticing that Susannah had left.

Outside, Susannah looked around for Brent, but didn't spot him. The only person she saw was Wally, who was working on the *Leif*.

Susannah walked over to the spacecraft. "How's it going?" she asked.

"Almost done," Wally grunted. "I'm just repairing the heat shield here. It got a bit charred when we entered Openworld's atmosphere faster than anticipated."

"Have you seen Brent?" she asked.

Wally nodded. "He's inside the living quarters with Doc and Angie," he said. "Having a physics lesson."

"Oh." Susannah and Brent had regular lessons—both on the group's computers and from the scientists themselves. Sometimes they studied together, but there were subjects where they were on different levels. Physics was definitely one of those subjects. Brent seemed to understand concepts with almost no instruction. Susannah was able to grasp what Doc talked about but found the subject of little interest. So she had no great desire to interrupt and chance being invited to participate.

"I have to get water," she explained to Wally. "Is it OK to take one of the rovers?"

"Fine with me," said Wally.

Susannah waited for Wally to tell her she couldn't go alone. But he had already turned back to the *Leif*. She shrugged. Surely it wouldn't hurt to get water by herself. And she would have a rover, so she wouldn't be gone for long.

Susannah loaded up the three passenger seats with empty water jugs and climbed in. She pressed a button and the rover's engine began to whir. Then she engaged the wheels and headed across the landscape for the water hole.

It was warm, and Susannah was perspiring by the time she drew up enough water to fill all the jugs. She put the heavy jugs into the rover, grateful that she was almost done. Then she straightened and wiped her brow. Her eyes surveyed the rocky area beyond. The ground rose gradually toward a ridge of hills that went on for some distance. The odd crystalline rocks of Openworld reflected Pele's light into various colors, almost as if they were a great prism. The scene was alien looking, but lovely.

Then Susannah froze. Something near the top of the hill had moved!

She shook her head. "I'm seeing things," she muttered

to herself. "The heat has gotten to me. Or it's a mirage or something."

Still, this wasn't the first time she had seen movement on Openworld. And in the same spot, too.

Susannah continued to stare out toward the ridge. And then she saw it again. Just a suggestion of movement—but there was definitely something out there.

She started forward, then stopped. What if she broke through the planet's surface again and disappeared into a sinkhole?

But what if I'm right and there *is* something out there? Susannah thought. We'd need to know that. Common sense told her to hurry back to the dome and let someone else worry about the matter. But curiosity made her decide not to.

Susannah walked a short distance past the water hole, carefully testing her weight with each step. Then she stopped and surveyed the landscape again.

There was definitely something there. On top of a large rock.

Susannah sank down on another rock to catch her breath—and to think. Whatever the object was, it was small. And it didn't seem at all threatening. Maybe she would just wait here and see what happened.

The moving object seemed to slide off the rock, then make its way closer to Susannah.

By now she could see it clearly. It was almost

shapeless—basically a gray mound about a foot across. It looked like it was covered with short, thick fur. But this fur seemed to vibrate constantly. And the creature didn't look like any furry animal Susannah had ever seen. It didn't even look like an animal. She couldn't identify eyes, or ears, or legs, or anything else familiar. In fact, all she could think of was a documentary she had seen once of undersea creatures that lived on coral reefs and spent their entire lives waving tentacle-like arms back and forth.

Susannah couldn't move—and she couldn't take her eyes off the thing. Is it as interested in me as I am in it? she wondered. Does it even know I'm here?

Something's Out There!

As if in reply, the creature moved a few inches forward—though Susannah couldn't see *how* it was moving. Then it hit her. No part of the creature was touching the ground. She could clearly see a foot of air beneath it. It was hovering above the surface of the planet!

Suddenly unnerved by this discovery, Susannah jumped to her feet. The creature darted off in the other direction. In a moment, it had disappeared over the crest of the ridge.

6

The Encounter

It wasn't until the creature had vanished from sight that Susannah thought about her communicator. She had been so stunned to see something moving—something alive. It hadn't even occurred to her to contact the others back at the dome.

She had never thought of her tazer, either. Of course, there hadn't been anything threatening about the creature. In fact, remembering it now, all she could think of was a large, dull gray powder puff. A large, dull gray powder puff that could hover in the air.

Shaking her head, Susannah walked back and got into the rover. As she steered it toward the dome, she thought about what she was going to tell the others. Would they believe what she told them? Did *she* even believe it?

Still, this wasn't the first time she had seen the object—or creature—or whatever it was. She had to convince the rest of them that she wasn't imagining things. They had to know.

"Hi! Want some help unloading the water?" called Brent as Susannah parked the rover.

"Yeah, that'd be great," she answered.

Brent reached into the backseat and pulled out a water jug. "Your mom'll have a fit when she finds out you went off on your own, you know."

"Hmmm . . ."

Brent paused to look at Susannah. "What's the matter? You're so pale. Did you almost crack up the rover?"

"No," Susannah said slowly, "but I have to talk to Doc. To all of you, actually. About something . . . something strange."

A few moments later, she was seated at the table in the living quarters of the dome. Everyone else gathered around.

"Now, tell us what you're worried about," said Doc.

Susannah hesitated, then took a deep breath. "I saw something alive out there, Doc. Something that moved."

"What?" chorused several voices.

"I saw something. In fact, this isn't the first time I've seen it."

Nelson's voice was cold. "You should have said something right away, Susannah. We depend on each other here. We all need to know what's going on."

"Wait a minute, Nelson," said Angie. "Susannah *did* say she had seen something earlier. The day she almost fell into the sinkhole. But I didn't believe her. So I think it's probably my fault she hasn't said anything."

Angie turned to Susannah. "Was it the same as what

you thought you saw before?"

Susannah nodded. "Yes. But this time I saw it much better, Angie. It practically came up to me. Then I moved and scared it."

Excited questions and comments came at Susannah from every direction. At last Doc held up a hand and said, "Quiet, everyone! Let the girl talk. Susannah, what did this thing look like?"

Susannah took a deep breath. "It was gray. Kind of blobby. But with something like fur all over its body."

"A gray blob," snorted Nelson. "Doesn't sound alive to me."

"It moved!" exclaimed Susannah. "It moved right toward me. Like it was as curious about me as I was about it." She went on to describe in great detail what she had seen.

"Well, that's quite a tale, Susannah," said Nelson when she finished.

"You don't believe me?" Susannah asked. "You think I'm lying?"

"I don't mean that—not at all," Nelson replied. "But you have to admit that your story isn't exactly logical. A furry gray blob that floats in the air and has no arms, legs, or eyes."

"It's not a story!" protested Susannah. "Why are you saying—"

Her mother's hand on her shoulder made Susannah

keep the rest of her question to herself. She wasn't surprised that Nelson was the one who was giving her a hard time. He didn't believe anything unless he saw it for himself. Besides, there was no point in arguing. She knew it wouldn't do for the colonists to start snapping at each other. Their safety depended on them working together and getting along.

Doc stood up. "OK, this is what we know," he said. "Susannah saw something and she's sure it's alive. That it's some sort of animal-like creature."

"So what we have to do is see it for ourselves," said Wally.

"Wally is right," added Angie. "We all need to know what we might be facing here. We're all affected."

"Agreed," said Doc. "We'll do some scouting for this creature." He looked at Susannah. "Susannah, you're the only one who's seen it, whatever it is. Are you willing to go out looking for it?"

"Of course. Doc, it didn't seem at all threatening. I don't think we need to be afraid of it."

"You don't *know* that, Susannah," said Nelson. "Not without proof."

Susannah wanted to shout at the man. To remind him that he didn't even believe the creature existed. So how could it possibly be dangerous? But she held her tongue.

"If Susannah is going, so am I," said Laura. "She's my daughter."

"That's fair," Doc said. "So you, Susannah, and I will go looking," he continued. "Nelson, I think you should come, too. Everyone else stays here for now." He looked around for approval. The others nodded slowly.

I wish Nelson wasn't coming, thought Susannah. But then she realized that Doc had his reasons. Nelson certainly wouldn't take *anyone's* word for it. He would have to see the creature for himself.

"We'll leave right after today's rain," Doc announced.

Several hours later, the scouting group got into a rover. First they drove the short distance to the sinkhole.

"Right over there," said Susannah, pointing to the ridge that rose slowly from the far side of the water hole. "That's where I saw it. Then it came down the hill until it was only about 5 feet away. And then it took off in the direction it had come from."

"I sure don't see any sign of a creature now," said Nelson. He stood with his hands on his hips and a look of disgust on his face.

"There isn't anything here now," Susannah admitted. "But it was here. It was!"

"OK, let's go a bit further afield," said Doc. "Susannah, you sit up front with me. Holler if you see anything."

The Encounter

They rode as far as the western border of the homestead, baking in the late afternoon sun. But there was no sign of anything but blue rocks, strange crystalline deposits, and crumbly blue soil.

Pele began to lower in the sky. Soon it would be sunset. "We'd better get back before it gets dark," said Doc.

"Now you don't believe me either, do you?" asked Susannah in a small voice.

"I believe you think you saw something, Susannah. And we'll look for it again tomorrow."

Susannah had to be satisfied with that. She sat back, trying to ignore Nelson's grumblings about a wasted afternoon.

The next few days passed without a sighting. Susannah was beginning to question herself. Maybe she had just managed to convince herself that someone—or something—had been waiting for them here. Maybe she hadn't really seen anything at all.

The rest of the group certainly seemed to share that opinion. Brent had even joked about seeing a "fur ball" on a rock. When Susannah had whirled around to look, he had laughed and said, "Gotcha!"

Nelson hardly talked to Susannah at all. Not that that was unusual. And Wally and Angie treated her as if she were an invalid. Someone to be catered to and treated gently. Someone not quite all there mentally.

Susannah wished she had never mentioned the

creature. Never seen the thing.

It was four days after her sighting. To Susannah's relief, no one had mentioned the creature all morning.

Brent called to Susannah. "Hey, want to come along? We're going to check out some of those crystal structures on the western side of the homestead."

"Sure," Susannah replied. "Who else is going?"

"Nelson, of course," responded Brent. "He's kind of our official geologist, after all."

Susannah almost changed her mind about going. But she was anxious to do something. Sitting around watching plants grow was pretty boring.

"Fine," she said.

The three of them got into the rover. Nelson automatically got into the driver's seat. Brent sat next to him, and Susannah crawled into the back.

As they bumped over the rocky ground, Susannah half-listened to the conversation in the front seat. Brent was asking Nelson questions about the terrain, the crystals, and how the rover worked. Nelson was answering in great detail. Nelson always seems to enjoy Brent, thought Susannah. Perhaps because they both spend every waking moment thinking about scientific things.

Then she caught a few words about the rover's radar. She leaned forward. "Does the radar pick up small things?" she asked.

"It could pick up a mosquito!" declared Nelson. "Provided there was one here, of course." He leaned over and pushed a button. Then he pointed to a computer screen on the front control panel. "There, it's on now. You can see it's indicating that big rock over there, and the ridge, and . . ."

Susannah wasn't sure why Nelson had stopped mid-sentence. Then Brent shouted, "There's something moving! The radar picked something up!"

Susannah's heart began to beat wildly. "I told you!" she shouted. "I told you!"

"Shhh!" ordered Nelson. He began to fiddle with buttons and dials. "There's something there, all right." He pointed to the screen. A shape hovered there, shifting and moving slightly.

"How big is it?" asked Brent nervously.

"Hard to say," replied Nelson. "I'd guess it's about 4 feet across."

Four feet! thought Susannah. "That's a lot bigger than the creature I saw," she said.

"Well, maybe that one was only a baby," said Brent.

"Hang on," Nelson ordered. Instead of weaving among the rocks, he steered the rover straight ahead—making a beeline for the spot on the radar screen.

Just then, the image on the radar screen shifted to the right.

"It's changing direction!" Nelson grumbled, spinning the steering wheel to the right. But no sooner had he done so than the image moved in yet another direction. Then another.

"I can't keep up with it," Nelson complained. "I'd better put the rover on remote and let it do the driving." He flicked a switch and took his hands from the steering wheel. Suddenly the rover was driving itself, chasing the image on the radar screen. The little vehicle banged across the rough ground, hurtling first one way and then another. Despite her safety belt, Susannah was bounced clear off her seat a couple of times. She hung on tightly with both hands.

The rover charged over a ridge and down a short slope. Then it came to a sudden stop in a small ravine.

"What happened?" Susannah gasped.

"I overrode the remote," Nelson said. He was studying the radar screen uneasily. "There's something just ahead. More than one something."

Susannah glanced at the radar screen. The single large blip that they had been pursuing was now a line of blips. She looked out over the landscape. "But I don't see anything there," she said.

"I think they're just over the ridge. Get your tazers out," Nelson ordered.

Hands shaking, Susannah obeyed. Everything around them was quiet—until . . .

"I hear something!" Brent exclaimed. "It sounds like some kind of motor."

"Shhh!" said Nelson. "I hear it, too!"

Just then, Susannah saw a blurry motion ahead of the rover. It was a creature like she had seen before—but not just one—a line of them. All coming over the ridge, shoulder to shoulder. Except that they didn't actually have shoulders. The sound was coming from the creatures. Not as soft as a purr. Not as loud as a roar. A kind of "churring" noise.

"Wait!" cried Susannah as Nelson raised his tazer. "They haven't done anything to us yet."

"I'm just ready to defend myself," said Nelson coldly.

"They worry me, Susannah," muttered Brent. She saw that he also held his tazer ready.

The line of creatures paused at the crest of the ridge.

"They're flying!" exclaimed Brent. "They're not touching the ground at all!"

"Actually, they seem to be hovering," corrected Nelson. "Interesting."

Then the creatures began to move forward, still in an unbroken line. They were about 7 or 8 feet away now, and they appeared to be hanging motionless in the air. A chill ran through Susannah. Had she been wrong? Were these creatures dangerous?

Nelson raised his tazer.

"Don't!" begged Susannah. "You don't know what might happen. Stunning one of these creatures might kill it! Or make them angry enough to attack us!"

Nelson ignored her. His finger pressed down on the tazer's ignition button. There was a loud, crackling sound, and a rock just in front of the creatures jerked in response to the blast. The creatures began to mill about, moving in confused circles.

Suddenly there was a second loud, crackling sound. Nelson dropped the tazer, staring at it in disbelief. A thin wisp of smoke rose from one end of the device.

The Encounter

"They fried my tazer!" shouted Nelson. One hand grabbed for the smoking tazer, the other reached for the starter button of the rover. The engine roared to life.

There was yet another crackling sound. This time it came from the rover itself. A bright flash lit up the radar screen; then the screen went black. The engine whined and died.

Nelson tried to restart the rover. Nothing happened. "They shorted the engine out, too!"

Then Susannah realized that someone was screaming. It was Brent.

Emergency Plans

As Brent's scream echoed off the rocks, the creatures slipped over the ridge and disappeared from sight.

Susannah lunged toward the front seat. "What's the matter? Brent! Are you OK?"

At the same time, Nelson grabbed Brent by the shoulder and turned him so they were facing. "What's wrong?" he asked.

"I can't see!" Brent cried. "I can't see!"

Nelson checked the boy over from head to foot. "OK, Brent, calm down," he said in measured tones. "I don't see any sign of injury. I think those things short-circuited your vision unit. Along with the rover and my tazer."

Brent drew in a long, ragged breath. "Sorry," he murmured. "I didn't mean to sound like a scared baby. It's just that all of a sudden everything went black."

"That would scare anyone," said Susannah.

Nelson turned slightly. His eyes met Susannah's. "I owe you an apology," he said. "Those creatures were exactly like the one you described."

Susannah shrugged. "I guess I can see why you thought I was nuts."

"I think we'd better get out of here," Nelson suggested. "We have to get back to the dome to warn the others. And to see what can be done about Brent's vision unit and the other devices that got fried."

"What do you mean by 'warn the others'?" asked Susannah with concern. "You don't think the creatures are dangerous, do you? They didn't hurt us."

"I don't consider having my vision unit destroyed exactly a friendly move," retorted Brent.

"But maybe they didn't realize what it was for," said Susannah. "Maybe they were just protecting themselves and ended up destroying all our machines."

"You may be right, Susannah," said Nelson. "At least about destroying everything." He pushed a button on his communicator. "This is dead, too."

Brent fumbled sightlessly at his wrist. He managed to find and push the "send" button. Nothing happened. Meanwhile, Susannah was making the same discovery about her own communicator.

"I assume your tazers are out of commission as well," commented Nelson.

Susannah picked up her tazer and aimed it at a nearby rock. When she activated the device, nothing happened. It was the same story with Brent's tazer.

"OK," said Nelson. "We have to get out of here. And that means we have to walk."

"Are we going to abandon the rover?" asked Brent.

"Unless you want to push it all the way back to the

dome," said Nelson. "Someone can come back later to try to repair it. The computer systems at the dome will have been tracking us, so we'll be able to find this spot again. And, if we're really lucky, someone will get curious about why we've stopped and come looking for us."

The three started out for the dome. Brent walked between Nelson and Susannah. He guided himself by keeping one hand on Nelson's arm. Susannah warned him when there was an obstacle in their path.

On foot, the trip seemed to take forever. The harsh, bright sun beat down on them. Then at last they heard something in the distance.

"Are more of the creatures coming?" asked Brent nervously.

"I don't think so," said Susannah.

"It sounds more like a rover engine," added Nelson. "Maybe it's our rescue party."

Sure enough, a moment later a rover appeared over the crest of a small hill. Doc was driving.

The rover came to a halt. "What happened?" asked Doc. "All of a sudden the computer lost your image. Did the rover break down? Is anyone hurt? Brent, you look upset. Are you OK?"

"My vision unit got wrecked, Gramps," said Brent. "But I'm fine."

"How could your—" Doc sputtered.

But Nelson interrupted. "Get us back to the dome and

we'll tell you everything," he said. "And believe me, Doc, there's plenty to tell."

Doc didn't ask any more questions. He helped his grandson into the backseat of the rover. Susannah sat next to Brent, and Nelson got into the front passenger seat. In silence, Doc steered the rover back to the dome.

Fifteen minutes later, the entire group was gathered together to hear the story. Brent was wearing an old vision unit. He was relieved to be able to see again, even if his vision was far less acute than with the experimental unit.

"Now, tell us what happened," Doc said.

Nelson looked at Susannah. "I think you should tell the story," he said. "After all, you saw them first."

"Them?" asked Angie. "You mean there really *are* creatures living on this planet?"

"Let Susannah explain," said Nelson, settling back in his chair.

She told the whole story, from the time the radar picked up the creatures until they disappeared over the hill.

"They short-circuited everything?" asked Doc.

"Everything," stated Nelson.

"This isn't good news," said Wally. "All we need is a bunch of hostile aliens."

"Hey, wait a minute!" exclaimed Susannah. "*We're* the aliens! These creatures lived here before we arrived. This is *their* home."

She turned to Nelson. "Besides, you saw what they

were like, Nelson. They weren't hostile. They didn't threaten us. They just ruined some machines."

Doc rose to his feet, sighing as if he felt every one of his sixty-plus years. "You're forgetting something, Susannah," he said. "We depend on machines to survive here. Without them, we're in trouble." He headed for the entryway.

"What are you doing?" asked Wally.

"I'm going to shut down our radio communication with Earth," said Doc. "Just as a precaution. I don't want that destroyed."

"Are you going to send a message about these creatures first?" asked Angie.

Doc shook his head. "I don't know enough yet," he said. "I'll just send word that we have technical difficulties. That we may be out of contact for a while."

Everyone watched as Doc left the dome. Susannah was relieved that he didn't seem to be panicking. That he wasn't sending word to Earth that they were being attacked by dangerous extraterrestrials. Still, the thought that the creatures could destroy their communications satellite worried her. It was the only link they had with Earth.

They were all still sitting there when Doc returned. "What's our next step, Doc?" asked Laura.

"That's easy! We have to capture one of these things!" exclaimed Nelson.

"Capture it? Why?" asked Angie.

"To study it, of course," replied Nelson. "Think of what an extraordinary opportunity this is! To study an alien being up close. Why, who knows what we might learn." His eyes gleamed with excitement.

"I'm not so sure we should do that," said Wally. "We don't want to make them angry. They might fry all our computer systems. Without computers, we'd be in trouble. It would mean that if we decided we had to leave Openworld, we wouldn't be able to."

"I still don't think they're dangerous," protested Susannah. "I think they're just curious. And if they hadn't been frightened by Nelson's tazer, they might not have done anything."

"Perhaps not, Susannah," said Doc. "But I do agree with Nelson. We have to learn more about these creatures. We have to find out whether or not they are dangerous. And just as importantly, whether or not they are intelligent beings."

"Well, *I* agree with Susannah," Brent said. "I think we should leave these churrs alone."

"Churrs?" echoed Doc.

Brent shrugged. "We have to call them something. And that's as good a name as any, isn't it? It's the sound they make. Kind of a cross between a purr and a growl."

"Churrs—or whatever you want to call them—hardly look intelligent, Doc," said Nelson. "They're just as Susannah first described them. Big, furry blobs."

"Big, furry blobs that have the power to short out anything computerized," Doc reminded him. "That have the power to trap us here."

He looked at his fellow colonists. "We have a few extra tasks now. First I'm going to ask Wally to check out the communicators and tazers to see if they can be fixed. If they can't, we have a few extras on hand. However, no one is to use any kind of computerized device in the presence of one of these creatures. We're not going to risk having anything else destroyed.

"And, from now on," Doc continued, "everyone is to stay in sight of the dome unless I know you're going farther. And no one—no one—takes off alone. Is that understood?"

There were nods all around the table. Then Doc sighed. "Tomorrow morning, Wally and I will go out and tow the rover back here so we can fix it. And after that, Nelson, we'll make a plan for capturing one of these creatures. We have to know what we're dealing with here. We have to."

8

The Churr Hunt

"**H**ere's my plan," Nelson explained the next morning. "I don't know whether they can actually control it or not, but the churrs are obviously able to give off some kind of energy. Correct me if I'm wrong, Wally, but isn't the lightsail netting full of little computer chips that sense energy?"

"Well, it's a bit more complicated than that," said Wally. "But basically, you're right."

"And when energy hits the sail, whether it's from a laser beam or just sunlight, some chips reflect energy back to the ship. Right?"

Wally nodded. "More or less."

"OK," said Nelson. "So if we hold a piece of lightsail netting up in front of these creatures, it'll probably reflect energy waves right back at them."

"Won't that make them mad?" Angie asked.

"I hope so," Nelson replied. "They might short out the chips or they might run away from them. Either way, they'll be confused. And, if we move fast, we should be able to catch one."

"How?" asked Wally. "You're not just going to grab one, are you?"

"I'm not touching one until we know more about them," said Nelson. "I figured we'd catch it in this." He held up a primitive net made from strips of gauze, woven together and attached to a stick.

Susannah struggled to keep from laughing. Here they were, light-years from Earth, talking about catching an extraterrestrial with a homemade net.

Doc shook his head. "I don't know, Nelson. It seems like we'd need something a bit more . . . technical to catch one of these creatures."

"Well, it's worth a try," said Nelson stubbornly. "Besides, high-tech isn't the way to go when you're trying to capture something that can destroy anything computerized."

"You have a point," sighed Doc. "OK. Let's give your plan a try."

"I want Susannah to come with us," said Nelson. "For some reason, they've appeared to her twice. So maybe she'll be our good luck charm."

"Susannah?" asked Doc.

"I'll go if you want me to, Doc," replied Susannah. "But you know that I don't think we should capture any of them."

"Objection noted," said Doc. "But I would like you to come. And Laura, as well."

"Why can't I come?" asked Brent. "They've appeared to me, too."

"No," said Doc firmly. "There's a chance that they would destroy the vision unit you're using now, Brent. And I haven't been able to fix the other one yet. I want you to stay as far away from these creatures as possible.

"Now," he continued, "let's get this show on the road."

The four of them walked outside where the rovers were parked. The vehicle Nelson had been driving when they met the creatures had been towed back to the dome. Wally had already started working on it, trying to repair the computers that controlled it.

They climbed into the functional rover. Minutes later, they were bumping over the rocky ground. And hours later, they returned to the dome without having sighted a single churr.

"We'll try again tomorrow," Doc announced.

The next day, the same group went out again. Again, there was no churr sighting. The following afternoon, Doc and Nelson went out with Angie. The day after that, they took Wally along.

The rover raced back to the dome late in the day. Susannah and the others who had stayed behind hurried up to the vehicle, anxious to hear the group's report.

"We saw one!" announced Doc. Susannah could see the excitement in the old scientist's eyes. Even if the churrs were a bit frightening, the experience of seeing an extra-terrestrial being was something Doc would enjoy.

"But you didn't capture it, I see," commented Angie.

"No," laughed Wally. He went on to explain that as soon as the rover's radar detected movement, they had parked the vehicle and gone off on foot. "We didn't want them near the rover," he said. They had soon found a small group of churrs. Doc and Wally had held up the lightsail netting. And, as Nelson had predicted, the netting had reflected energy back at the churrs. But when Nelson slipped the net over a churr, it simply flattened itself into a thin disk shape, slipped out from under, and took off.

"So we're back to the drawing board," sighed Nelson. "There has to be some way to capture one of these things."

"Doc, did you think they seemed dangerous?" asked Susannah. She held her breath as she waited for an answer.

Doc hesitated before replying. At last, he said, "I don't know, Susannah. They certainly didn't try to harm us. However, I just don't know."

"But if they don't try to harm us, we shouldn't try to harm them, right?"

Doc put a hand on Susannah's shoulder. "Right, Susannah. And we'll try not to. I promise."

Susannah felt comforted by Doc's words. Still, she couldn't help wondering if they hadn't already somehow harmed the churrs. Just by coming to their planet. Just by being here.

For the next few days, a churr-hunting expedition left the dome every day. And every day it came back empty-handed. Several times churrs were spotted, but they fled as soon the humans got near. No one got close enough to attempt a capture.

Gradually, things began to settle down. The colonists had plenty of work to do. So those who weren't actually hunting churrs got back to their normal tasks.

For Susannah, this meant helping her mother. Laura was investigating the strange mosslike plants that grew on Openworld. So, as they had been doing for days, the two of them headed out in the morning to gather samples.

"I've been wondering about something, Mom," Susannah said as she dug up a plant. She shook the blue dirt off the shallow roots. "You know how some of these plants are in beds that are shaped like triangles and stuff?"

"Yes."

"Well, I was just wondering—do you think the churrs planted them that way?"

Laura sat back on her heels and considered her daughter's question. "I don't know, Susannah," she said at last. "It seems odd to think that a creature with no arms and legs could plant a garden. But . . ."

"But what?" asked Susannah when her mother hesitated.

"But we're a long way from Earth. So odd things can

happen. I won't say it's impossible that these are gardens of some sort. Just that it's unlikely."

"Well, I think they planted them."

"And you may be right. But we have no proof of that yet."

"I know," replied Susannah grudgingly. "Sometimes I get sick of having to prove everything. Of always being told to think like a scientist. Sometimes it would be nice to just believe."

Laura laughed. "I know, sweetie. And that's one of the things I love about you. You have the courage to just believe things. Your dad was the same way, and he was also a talented scientist."

A warm glow filled Susannah. It was good to know that she was like her father. And that it was possible to be both a scientist and someone who could believe in things that couldn't necessarily be proven.

That afternoon, after the usual rain, Laura made a request. "I really need more of this ferny plant we found, Susannah. Could you and Brent dig up another sample?"

"Sure. But Brent is busy. He and Doc are working on fixing his vision unit. The experimental one. Is it OK for me to go on my own?"

Laura brushed her curly hair off her forehead with a dirty hand. "Oh, I think so. You'll be in sight of the dome. And it's not like a churr has come that close, anyway. So if it doesn't make you nervous, go ahead. Just be sure to come right back when you're done."

The Churr Hunt

"I will," said Susannah.

She left the dome carrying a small trowel and a bag to hold the sample. The air was clear and fresh, as it always was after the rain. Susannah breathed deeply, grateful to be outside. Then she headed to one side of the dome, where the fernlike plants grew in a thick bed.

Susannah walked along the side of a hilly ridge, inspecting the plants. She was looking for a section of leaves that appeared to grow wild. If the churrs were gardeners, she didn't want to disturb their work any more than she had to.

At last she saw what she wanted. A clump of fernlike leaves grew at the edge of a large blue rock. Susannah knelt by the stone. She put the trowel down and ran the fingers of one hand under the leaves, looking for the main part of the stem.

Her hand touched something odd. She jerked her arm back.

Then she parted the leaves. A churr lay underneath.

9

Dead or Alive?

Susannah bit back a cry of surprise. It was a very small churr. Smaller than the one she had first seen.

She leaned closer to observe the creature more carefully. It wasn't moving. Even its furry coat was still. In fact, the fur looked paler than usual, and it lay almost flat against the ground.

Susannah realized that she had been holding her breath. She let it out now in a great sigh. Was the churr sick? Was it dead?

Gingerly, she touched the creature again with one finger. It felt neither cold nor warm—it was pretty close to the temperature of the air, she thought. The fur was scratchy under her fingers. Sort of like the bristles of a hairbrush.

Suddenly a few strands of fur quivered slightly. Susannah snatched her hand back quickly. She watched as a shudder passed over the creature. Then it was still.

"You *are* sick!" she whispered. She didn't know what to do. Should she leave the churr here? If she did, would it die? Should she take it to the dome so Nelson could examine it and perhaps give it some medicine? And if she did that, would it die?

Susannah looked down at her wrist. She could use her communicator to call her mother and ask for advice. But they had all promised not to use computerized devices if they were anywhere near a churr.

Susannah pulled the leafy stems back so she could watch the churr closely. For the most part, it lay still. However, every minute or so, another shudder passed over the creature, rippling its fur slightly. Susannah wished she knew more about it. Was it breathing? Was it simply sleeping? Or was it dying?

She raised her eyes to study the landscape. There was nothing in sight but rocks, crystalline mounds, and dirt. All of it blue. All of it empty.

Her decision was made. She couldn't leave the churr here. Not all by itself. She untied the scarf she wore at the neck of her jumpsuit and smoothed it out on the ground. Then, ever so carefully, she slid her hands under the churr. It was like lifting a pile of feathers—the churr seemed to weigh next to nothing.

Susannah gently placed the churr on her scarf. Then she slipped the trowel into her pocket. She gathered up the corners of the scarf, enfolding the churr. She got to her feet slowly, taking one last look around for signs of another churr. There were none.

Susannah walked very slowly back to the dome,

holding the scarf and its contents away from her body. She went through the entryway and straight to the lab area. Her mother was bent over a flat of seeds. Wally was in a far corner, working on a damaged communicator.

Laura looked up. "That didn't take long," she said. Then she looked at the scarf in Susannah's hand. "But why did you wrap the plant up in your scarf?"

"It's not a plant, Mom," said Susannah. She placed the scarf on the table and folded back the edges.

Dead or Alive?

"My goodness!" exclaimed Laura. "Where did you find it? No, don't tell me yet. Wally! Get Doc and the others in here right away!"

Something in her tone of voice kept Wally from asking questions. In a matter of moments, he had located the others and brought them to Laura and Susannah.

They all had the same reaction—stunned silence.

Nelson spoke first. "How did you capture it?"

"I didn't," replied Susannah. "I found it under a bushy plant. I think it's sick. Can you help it, Nelson?"

He leaned forward, studying the churr. "I don't know, Susannah," he said. "I didn't learn anything about treating churrs in medical school."

"It doesn't look alive, anyway," said Brent.

"It was," said Susannah. "I think it still is. Every once in a while the fur moves a little." As she finished speaking, the churr shuddered once more. "See! It *is* alive!"

She looked up at Doc. "Was I wrong to bring it back here, Doc? Should I have left it where I found it?"

"I don't know, Susannah," the scientist said. "But I do know that Nelson will try to help it if he can. Now I think we should all let him get to work."

"Brent, go and get my bag," Nelson ordered. "I don't want to move the thing again."

Brent hurried off for the bag. The others backed away, giving Nelson some room. But no one left the area. They all wanted to see what happened.

Nelson gently prodded and poked the creature. "It seems to have a respiratory system somewhat like an amphibian's," he said in a low voice. "I think it breathes through its skin."

He continued to examine the creature. "No sign of any external injury."

The churr shuddered again, its fur waving like a field of grain blowing in the wind. Then it was still.

That was the last time it moved. After fifteen minutes of examination, Nelson straightened up. "I think it's dead," he announced in a solemn voice.

Susannah felt hot tears well up in her eyes. She dashed them away with her fists. "Do you think we killed it somehow?" she asked.

Her mother put her arms around her. "We don't know that, honey," she said. "Churrs may get sick and die just like people do. It might have nothing at all to do with us."

Doc sighed. "Well, Nelson, you have a churr to study now. I'm just sorry it's not a live one."

"Let's start by scanning its body," Nelson suggested. Laura hurried to get a hand-held scanner and connect it to her computer.

Nelson passed the scanner over the churr. An image appeared on the computer monitor. There wasn't much to see—just a strange tangle of purple lines.

"I don't see any sign of organs like animals have on Earth," murmured Nelson. "No heart or lungs or anything else recognizable."

Dead or Alive?

"Are those lines blood vessels?" asked Susannah.

"I don't think so," Nelson said. "I'm not sure we can even compare these creatures to anything that lives on Earth. But I think the lines may be some kind of nervous system."

"Then where is its brain?" asked Brent.

"I can't see any sign that it has much of one," Nelson announced. "So I think we can be sure it's not intelligent."

Nelson sounded very sure of himself, but Susannah couldn't help wondering. The churrs had seemed pretty organized when they appeared over the ridge. And there were the signs she had seen of gardens that had been planted. Could all that be due to some kind of animal instinct? Wouldn't it require a measure of intelligence?

Nelson turned off the scanner. "I can probably find answers to some of our questions by dissecting it," he said.

Susannah didn't like the idea of Nelson cutting the churr open, but she knew that dissection was a valuable tool for doctors. Still, she didn't want to think about it.

Nelson gathered up the churr and headed for the infirmary, in a far corner of the lab area. Meanwhile, Doc turned to Brent. "Come on," he said, "a few more adjustments and I think you can have your good vision unit back."

"I can't wait," replied Brent. "And at least I know a dead churr can't destroy it." Then he looked at Susannah's face. "I'm sorry, Susannah," he said. "I'm not glad it's dead. Really, I'm not."

"I know," she said softly.

Doc and Brent went off to finish their work. So did the others. Susannah stood by her mother's worktable. "I guess I should go back and get the plant you wanted," she said. "I don't want to be here while Nelson is dissecting the churr."

She glanced toward Nelson's work area. A screen hid the infirmary from the rest of the laboratory. Still, she knew what would be going on behind it.

Before she could leave, Brent and Doc reappeared. Brent was wearing his original vision unit. A big smile stretched across his face.

"Success!" announced Doc.

"Yeah, it's even better than it was before," added Brent. He looked up at his grandfather. "Can I watch Nelson dissect the churr?"

"If it's OK with him," Doc replied.

"What about you, Susannah?" asked Brent.

"No!" exclaimed Susannah.

"OK, OK, I was just asking." Brent started toward the infirmary area. But halfway there, he stopped. He stood and stared intently at the screen that shielded Nelson and the churr from the others.

"What?" he muttered. He shook his head. Then he reached up and touched his vision unit, settling it more firmly in place.

He ran toward the screen, calling out, "Nelson! Stop!"

10

Reclaimed

As Susannah, Doc, and Laura all rushed after Brent, the screen that separated the infirmary from the rest of the lab swept back.

Nelson stood there, scalpel in hand. He looked at Brent as if the boy had lost his mind. "What are you yelling about?" he asked impatiently.

"It's alive!" Brent exclaimed. "The churr is alive!"

Nelson turned back to study the churr, which lay motionless on the examining table. "It's not alive," he said. "It hasn't moved at all."

"I can see a glow around it," Brent insisted. "I'm sure it means the thing is alive."

"That's nonsense."

"No, it's not! You know this vision unit lets me see a range of light that the human eye can't. It did before, and it seems to be even more powerful now."

"Nelson, Brent is right about that," Doc said. "So let's not be too hasty about cutting this creature up."

"We can't cut it!" added Susannah. "Not if there's any chance that it's alive. That would be murder!"

"Don't get hysterical, Susannah," snapped Nelson. "I'm not going to kill the thing. It's already dead, I tell you." He turned to Brent. "Maybe you *do* see a glow, Brent. But it's probably just leftover energy. There is no sign that the thing is alive now."

"No sign that *we* recognize," said Susannah.

"Besides, it's more than a glow, Nelson," Brent said. He stared intently at the churr. "It . . . It . . . Well, it sort of pulses. It's very slow, but the glow definitely gets stronger, then weaker, then stronger. Almost like breathing."

Brent turned his back on the churr. "I don't want to look at the thing. It's alive, I tell you. And if you make it angry, it might destroy my vision unit again."

Doc stepped forward. He grabbed a corner of the screen and pulled it shut to hide the churr. "We have to talk about what to do. From what Brent says, we can't be sure the thing isn't alive. And if it is, we certainly don't want to be responsible for harming it."

Susannah breathed a sigh of relief. She should have known that Doc would be reluctant to hurt a living thing. No matter how much he wanted to learn about it.

Doc interrupted her thoughts. "Susannah, would you go and get the others? We need to have a meeting."

Soon all the colonists gathered around the long table in the living quarters. "All right," Doc said, "you know why we're here. We need to discuss what to do about this churr."

"I say we keep it here to study it," said Nelson. "And to see if it really is alive."

"Well, I think we should get rid of it," commented Angie. "It makes me nervous having it around."

"It makes me nervous, too," said Brent. "What if it

suddenly recovers and decides to wipe out my vision unit—and all the computers?"

"I agree that we should let it go," said Susannah. "But not because I'm worried about what it might do. Because I should have left it where I found it. Maybe other churrs would have come to take care of it. Maybe they still can help it."

"Laura and Wally—we haven't heard from you," Doc said. "What are your feelings?"

Laura reached out and covered Susannah's hand with her own. "I agree with Susannah," she said. "I don't think the churr is going to hurt us. But I do think there's a chance that we might hurt it. I think we should put it back where Susannah found it."

"So do I," replied Wally.

"This is silly," complained Nelson in an angry voice. "We're supposed to be scientists. We should keep this thing here to study."

"Sorry, Nelson, but you're outvoted," Doc said calmly. He turned to Susannah. "Do you remember exactly where you found the churr?"

Susannah nodded.

"OK, then, I'll go with you to return it."

Doc went into the infirmary area. A moment later he returned with the churr in his arms, Susannah's scarf still wrapped around it. The two of them headed for the door. Laura and Wally followed them. Brent moved to the window to watch.

"Wait!" Brent shouted as Doc's hand reached for the door handle.

"What is it, Brent?" asked Doc. "I don't think you should come with us."

"I don't want to. But there's something out there, Gramps. Churrs, I think. Lots of them."

"What makes you say that?"

Brent's voice shook slightly as he answered. "I can see a glow. All along the horizon. Just like the glow I saw from the churr that Susannah found. Only a lot brighter."

Doc handed the churr to Susannah, who cradled it in her arms.

"Everyone stay put," Doc ordered. "I want to see if I can spot anything out there."

"Take a tazer!" called Angie.

"Why?" said Nelson bitterly. "It would be no use against these things."

Ignoring the exchange, Doc pulled the door open. As soon as he did, they could all hear it. A low hum—no—a chorus of "churrs." The sound seemed to come from all directions.

Doc hesitated. "I don't see anything," he said. "But I hear them."

"We all do," said Laura.

"Doc, I still think I should take it back," Susannah said.

"You're not going out there now," Laura protested.

Susannah whirled and stared at her mother. "I thought

you agreed that they weren't dangerous," she said.

"I *think* they aren't," Laura responded. "But I don't know for sure."

Susannah looked down at the churr. It seemed to weigh even less than when she had first handled it. As she watched, a slight shudder made the creature's fur quiver.

"I have to, Mom," she said. "But I won't go all the way. I'll just put it outside the dome. We can see if the churrs come to get it. If they don't . . . If they go away—then I'll take it back to the spot where I found it."

Laura glanced at Doc, her concern obvious. The scientist's eyes were on Susannah. He nodded. "Come on," he said. "I'll come with you."

Doc opened the door all the way. The churring became louder. And then, as the pair walked out, churrs appeared in the distance. There was a long line of them to the west, coming from the direction of the water hole.

As if they knew what Susannah was doing, the churrs paused. She knelt by a large rock. Then, as Doc watched, she gently placed the small churr on the ground in the shade of the stone. She folded her scarf over the creature to offer it a bit more protection.

Then she moved back to stand beside Doc. Shading her eyes with one hand, she stared out at the churrs. "I think they'll come for it," she said softly.

Doc's hand gripped her shoulder. "I think you're right," he said. "We should get back to the dome now."

They turned and started walking. Doc glanced back over his shoulder once to see if the churrs had moved. Susannah just stared straight ahead.

"Thank goodness!" Laura exclaimed when they entered the dome. She hugged her daughter close to her.

Angie, who had been watching out a window, called, "The things are moving!"

Everyone found a spot to watch. The churrs hovered in the air, advancing toward the small churr in an unbroken line. Their fur quivered as if a breeze were passing over them. The churring sound was now loud enough to be heard with the door closed.

Then the creatures surrounded the small churr. In a matter of minutes, they retreated. The little creature was gone. All that remained was a bright spot against the blue rock—Susannah's scarf.

11

The Rescue

After that, there was a sort of truce between the churrs and the humans. This was mainly because there were no churr sightings. And because the colonists stayed close to the dome.

One evening, as the group ate dinner, Nelson raised a question. "Should we be trying to communicate with Earth again, Doc? To warn them about the churrs?"

Doc didn't answer right away. At last he said, "I've been thinking about that, Nelson. But I don't want to start a panic. We still really don't have any evidence that the churrs are dangerous."

"Shouldn't we at least mention them?" Nelson asked.

"I don't know," Doc said slowly. "I'd rather wait."

The expression on Nelson's face indicated that he disagreed. However, he didn't say anything more about the matter.

As days passed without incident, the colonists began to relax a bit. One morning, Susannah and Brent headed outside, not far from the dome. They had volunteered to check one of the experimental crops Laura had planted.

Several times a week, the plants were measured to see how fast they were growing.

"No sign of churrs," Brent said.

"Maybe they've moved farther away," Susannah suggested.

Something in her tone of voice made Brent look at her carefully. "That would be good, wouldn't it?" he asked.

"I don't know," Susannah said slowly. She realized that she had mixed feelings about the idea. On one hand, she was relieved that no real conflict had developed between the colonists and the churrs. On the other hand, she felt a sense of guilt.

"If they did move, it would be because of us," she said. "Because they don't feel safe around us."

Brent shrugged. "That's fine with me. I don't feel safe around them."

"But it doesn't seem fair," Susannah protested. "They were here first." She didn't say what she was really thinking. That it all seemed too much like what had happened long ago on Earth. When explorers had arrived in the "New World" and changed life forever for those who already lived there.

Several days later, after a morning of lessons, Susannah said, "I'm really tired of sticking so close to the dome."

"So am I," agreed Brent.

"There's been no sign of churrs," Susannah continued. "Or of any other kind of danger. Let's ask if we can go out this afternoon. Just to walk around and explore the homestead. I've hardly been past the water hole in ages."

When they made their request, the adults hesitated. But at last Doc said, "I suppose there's no harm in it. We've checked out the immediate area and haven't found anything dangerous. Just be sure you have your communicators. In fact, I want you to use them to check in with us every half hour."

"And you have to promise that you'll head back here at the first sign of anything unusual," insisted Laura.

"We promise," the two friends said in one voice.

Half an hour later, Susannah clicked off her communicator. She had just checked in with her mother, reporting that she and Brent were somewhere northwest of the water hole.

Now they stood and surveyed the land to the south. "It all pretty much looks the same, doesn't it?" Susannah said. "Just rocks and rounded hills."

"Yeah," agreed Brent. "There are no real mountains and valleys like on Earth. Of course, we've only seen a little bit of the planet. Imagine coming from Openworld to Earth and landing in the middle of the United States. You'd think there were no mountains and valleys there, either."

"That's true," said Susannah. "Do you suppose we'll ever get to explore more of Openworld?"

"I'm sure we will. As soon as we're more settled. Right now there's a lot to do just to be able to live where we are.

Besides, we need to know more about the churrs before we go too far."

"I suppose," said Susannah. "Come on. Let's at least walk to the south before we head back. I haven't been in that direction recently."

They set off with Brent in the lead. They hadn't gone far when he cried out.

"Ouch!"

"What's wrong?" Susannah asked. "Are you all right?"

"I'm fine," Brent said. "I just stubbed my toe on some dumb rock. Guess I'd better watch my step." He reached down to pick up the offending stone.

"This is odd," he said. "Different than any of the rocks we've seen so far."

Susannah looked down at the object in Brent's hand. It was a rounded half-circle of stone about 4 inches across. But it wasn't the usual blue color of most rocks on Openworld. It was a pale green.

"Brent," she said. "I don't think it's just a rock."

"What do you mean?"

"I mean it's been carved," said Susannah. "Look at it! You can see the marks where the stone has been cut away and then smoothed."

Brent turned the rock over in his hands. "Look at this!" he exclaimed. "There are some markings on the other side."

Together they studied the rock. Brent was right. Symbols were carved into the flat side of the stone.

"It's almost like some kind of writing," Susannah said.

"That's nuts! Who would be writing on stones on Openworld?"

Susannah hesitated before saying what she was thinking. "Maybe . . . Maybe it belongs to the churrs."

"Oh, come on, Susannah. You're saying the churrs have some sort of language?"

"They might!"

"That's ridiculous!" said Brent. "Nelson couldn't even find any sign that they even have brains! And I sure don't think that the churrs could be smart enough to have a written language. Now let's get going. I don't like it here."

He dropped the rock and strode off to the south. Before following, Susannah reached down to retrieve the green stone. She dropped it into her pocket.

They walked along in silence for a few minutes. Soon they had passed the water hole. Susannah realized that she had never been in this part of the homestead before. Not that it looked much different to her than what she had already seen.

She kept her eyes on the ground, hoping to find another carved stone. So she didn't realize that Brent had stopped until she crashed into him.

"Hey!" she cried.

"Shhh!"

Susannah looked at Brent. Beads of sweat had appeared on his forehead. His lips quivered.

"Brent, what's the matter?"

"You can't see it, can you?" he asked.

"See what?"

"The glow. It's all around us here. It started just past the water hole. But it took me a minute to realize what I was seeing."

"Glow? You mean—"

"I mean there must be churrs here," said Brent. "It's the same kind of light they give off." He stared into the distance uneasily.

"I don't see any," said Susannah. "Do you?"

Brent shook his head. "Let me concentrate for a minute, will you?"

Susannah was quiet. She watched her friend as he stared off in the distance. His vision unit hid his eyes, so she couldn't see his expression. But she could tell he wasn't happy.

"There's definitely something here," Brent said at last.

"Churrs, you mean?" Susannah swiveled her head, looking for some sign of the creatures.

"No," Brent replied. "Structures of some sort."

"What are you talking about? I can't see anything!"

Brent sighed. "I know. But I'm not crazy, Susannah. I can see a glow. It's faint. And when I really concentrate, I can see shapes. Towers and ramps and buildings. Most of them kind of broken down."

"What do you think it is?"

"It looks like a city. A small city."

"An invisible city," murmured Susannah. "At least invisible to me."

"I wonder . . ." Brent said thoughtfully. He turned around to face in the direction they had come. "Yes," he said. "Now I can see it. Now that I know what I'm looking for."

"What can you see?" asked Susannah impatiently.

"More broken-down buildings," said Brent. "I can even see where we have stepped on some of them. There's a trail of flattened structures right where we've walked."

Susannah looked down at her feet. "Oh no!" she exclaimed.

"This is creepy," muttered Brent. "I want to get out of here." He began to run.

"Wait!" shouted Susannah. But Brent kept on running. She had no choice but to follow. She didn't want to be alone.

They hadn't gone far before Brent fell again. This time he didn't get up immediately. Susannah ran to his side, breathing heavily. Brent was groaning and holding his leg.

"What is it?" Susannah asked.

"My ankle! I think I broke it!"

"Let me help you get up," Susannah said. "Maybe you just twisted it."

But trying to stand showed that Brent could be right. His ankle was severely injured. There was no way he was going to be able to walk back to the dome.

Susannah helped her friend sit down again; then she sank down beside him. "I'll call for help," she said. "Someone can come with a rover to pick us up." She reached for the button on her communicator.

"Wait!" said Brent in a hoarse whisper. "Don't turn it on right now."

Susannah looked up from her wrist. There were churrs hovering just beyond Brent. She looked over her shoulder. Churrs were there, as well. In fact, they were all around them. More churrs than she had ever seen at one time.

Brent reached up to touch the side of his vision unit. "What are you doing?" whispered Susannah.

"Turning it off. I'd rather be blind for now than have it destroyed again. But you'll have to be my eyes."

Susannah nodded. Then realizing that Brent couldn't see her, she said, "I will."

For a few minutes, no one moved—neither human nor churr. There was no sound, either, not even the usual noise the creatures made.

"What's happening?" asked Brent in a low voice.

"They're just watching us," explained Susannah. "Brent, we can't just sit here like this. I'm going to stand up now and see what they do."

Slowly, Susannah rose to her feet. As she did, the churring started. At first it was a low hum. It quickly grew to a loud, constant buzzing. Then the churrs started to move forward, closing the circle.

Susannah gasped and the creatures halted.

"What?" asked Brent in alarm.

"They were moving forward. But they stopped."

A long minute passed. Then the churrs moved forward again. Susannah didn't know what to do. She could try running through them, but that would mean leaving Brent behind.

The creatures kept coming. When they were a matter of inches from Susannah and Brent, they stopped hovering and settled on the surface of the planet. There they flattened themselves against the blue soil.

The only thing that moved was the gently rippling fur on the creatures' backs. The churring noise grew softer. To Susannah, it suddenly seemed an oddly comforting sound.

She studied the ring of churrs carefully. "I think they've got something in mind," she said.

"Like what?"

"I think they want to help us," Susannah said.

"Are you sure?"

"I'm not sure of anything."

Acting on instinct, Susannah sank down next to Brent. The churrs immediately began to move forward.

Susannah held her breath. What if she were wrong? What if the creatures meant to harm them?

Then the churrs were all around them. The first to reach Susannah and Brent flattened themselves even more. Susannah realized that they were sliding underneath her!

"Brent," she said softly. "Don't move. I think they're going to pick us up. Just like they did with the baby we put outside for them to find."

"Where are they going to take us?" asked Brent fearfully.

Susannah didn't have an answer to that question. Back to the dome, she hoped. But she certainly wasn't sure that was what the churrs had in mind.

Then she realized that she and Brent were rising. She shifted her weight carefully, feeling the bristly fur of churrs beneath her. The sensation was oddly familiar—like floating on an air-filled mattress in a swimming pool.

Before long, the churrs were about a foot off the ground. And Brent and Susannah were on top of them. On top of a living platform of churrs.

Slowly the platform turned and headed in the direction of the dome.

12

Next Steps

"What's happening?" asked Brent frantically. "What's going on?"

"They're helping us," said Susannah. "I'm sure of it now, Brent. They're headed back to the dome."

She looked at her friend. "Turn on your vision unit," she said in a low voice. "See for yourself."

When Brent hesitated, she said, "They're obviously not trying to hurt us, Brent. I think it's safe."

Slowly Brent lifted one hand toward his eyes. He drew a deep breath. Then his fingers found the controls to the unit. "It's on," he said.

He looked around. They were about two feet off the ground now and moving steadily. The top of the dome was visible over a ridge.

"What did I tell you?" asked Susannah with satisfaction. "They're taking us home."

"I guess so," murmured Brent.

As the churrs moved up and over the rise, Susannah heard something. The whirring of an engine. "Oh no!" she cried. "I should have tried to contact the dome. When we didn't check in, someone must have decided to come looking for us."

Just as she pressed the button to activate her communicator, a rover appeared in the distance. Halfway up the hill, it screeched to a sudden halt. Its wheels scattered blue stones in their wake. Susannah could see that Doc was at the wheel. Her mother sat at his side.

"Doc!" she whispered into the communicator. "Can you hear me?"

She could see the scientist lift his hand. Then his voice came through loud and clear. "Susannah?"

"They're helping us, Doc. Don't do anything. Just wait there."

She was too far away to read the expression on Doc's face. But she saw her mother reach over toward the rover's controls. The engine died at once. All that could be heard was a low, steady churring sound.

The platform of churrs began to descend gradually. When they were about 15 feet from the rover, the churrs settled gently to the ground. Immediately, they began to retreat, staying at first in the shape of a circle. An ever-widening circle that left Susannah and Brent isolated at its center.

Then, as if at some inaudible signal, the circle broke apart. The churrs hovered for a few moments, then turned and moved away. Soon they had all disappeared over the rocky ridge.

Shakily, Susannah got to her feet. At the same time, Doc and Laura hurled themselves from the rover and ran forward.

"Susannah, are you OK?" Laura called.

"Yes, but Brent hurt his ankle."

Doc reached Brent first. He knelt down and ran his hands over the boy's ankle. "I think it's broken," he said. "We'd better get you back so Nelson can set it for you."

He gathered Brent up in his arms and carried him to the rover. After settling his grandson in the backseat, he climbed in himself.

When Laura and Susannah were seated, Doc started the rover. Then, without looking at the two children, he asked, "What happened? Tell us everything."

Susannah's words tripping over Brent's, they told the whole story. The carved green stone. The glow. The invisible city. Brent's accident. The sudden appearance of the churrs. And the way the creatures had rescued them.

By the time the rover reached the dome, they had finished. Neither Doc nor Laura had much to say. Susannah followed them silently as Doc carried Brent into the dome.

Questioning eyes met them as they entered. However, no one said anything. Doc deposited Brent in the infirmary area. "Nelson, as soon as you've had a chance to see to Brent's ankle, we all need to talk."

A while later, Brent was seated at the table with a cast

on his leg. With Susannah's help, he repeated the story of their adventure. Once again, their tale was greeted with stunned silence. A silence that Wally was the first to break.

"So you're saying these churrs rescued you after Brent got hurt."

"They did!" said Susannah. "Mom and Doc saw it."

Laura nodded. "They did, Wally."

"But even more significant than that is what Brent saw," said Doc. "Signs of a ruined civilization."

"Certainly not one any of the rest of us can see," commented Nelson.

"No, that's right," replied Doc. "But that's not an issue. We already know that Brent's vision unit picks up light waves that the human eye can't see. If he says he saw broken-down buildings, he did. Besides, we *can* see the carved stone Brent found. And that is also a sign of some kind of civilized, creative being."

"So whose civilization was it?" said Angie. "Surely not the churrs'?"

"Why not?" asked Susannah. "Why couldn't it be theirs?"

"Come on, Susannah. How could they build anything? They don't even have arms or legs. And we haven't seen any sign of them using tools."

"Maybe there once was intelligent life on Openworld," suggested Laura.

Nelson got to his feet. "Yes. And maybe the churrs destroyed that civilization."

"You're the one who's always talking about proof," snapped Susannah. "There's absolutely no proof that the churrs did anything like that."

"And no proof that they didn't," retorted Nelson.

Doc spoke up before Susannah could reply. "All right," he said, "there is no point in arguing. What we have to do is *find* proof. Proof that the churrs once created a city—or that they destroyed one."

"And how are we supposed to find this proof, Doc?" asked Wally. "We certainly can't ask the churrs."

"No, we can't," agreed Doc. "But we can put together an exploratory mission. We haven't gone much beyond the homestead yet. I think it's time to do that. Perhaps we'll find something that answers some of our questions."

"I want to go," said Susannah.

"So do I," added Wally and Nelson at the same time.

"I'm sure everyone wants to go," said Doc. "Here's what I propose: We'll go in a few days. I want Brent's ankle to be stable before we leave. He and Susannah must be part of the mission. They seem to have some relationship with the churrs.

"I want three people to stay here at the dome," Doc continued. "Two more of us will go with Susannah and Brent in one of the rovers. This is merely a precaution. If the exploratory group runs into trouble, I want someone here to help them. If there are no volunteers willing to stay behind, we'll draw straws."

Everyone nodded. Then Doc pushed himself away

from the table and got to his feet. "OK, we have a lot to do. Brent and Susannah, would you please record everything you've observed about the churrs. Laura, I'd like you to work up a written plan for our expedition, based on what you learn from Susannah and Brent. Nelson and Angie, you're in charge of gathering supplies. And Wally, I need your help with a special project I've got in mind."

"What kind of project?"

Doc smiled. "Well, I guess you could say it's a secret weapon of sorts."

13

Unexpected Discoveries

Two days later, the expedition was ready. It was time to decide who was going and who was staying behind.

"I'll stay," Laura volunteered. "Susannah has to go. I want to be sure there's help if she—if anyone on this mission—needs it."

"Thank you, Laura," Doc said. He looked at the rest of the group. "Any other volunteers?"

No one spoke up and Doc smiled. "I know," he said. "I feel the same way. So let's draw straws."

A minute later it was done. Wally and Angie would be staying with Laura. Doc and Nelson would be joining Susannah and Brent.

"Before we leave," said Doc, "it's time to reveal our 'secret weapon.' Wally, if you wouldn't mind?"

Wally nodded and walked over to a shelf in Doc's work area. He took down a box and brought it over to Doc.

"Wally's been helping me with this project," Doc explained as he reached into the box. He pulled out what looked like safety goggles used by construction workers.

"What is it?" asked Nelson.

"A simplified version of Brent's vision unit," Wally said. "Doc figured out how to modify the design so it works with the human eye. No computer chip implant needed."

"So it will let someone see as well as Brent does?" asked Susannah.

"Not quite," Doc answered. "But it should allow you to see light waves that you wouldn't ordinarily be able to. Here, try it on," he said, handing the goggles to Susannah.

Susannah slipped the goggles on and gazed around the laboratory. Of course, there was no odd glow to see, but things did look sharper.

Doc reached into the box again. "There are goggles for you and me as well, Nelson. So we will all be able to see the same things." He handed one pair to Nelson and kept the other for himself.

"Time to go," Doc announced.

"Be careful," Wally said. "And don't forget to check in with us regularly."

"We won't," Doc promised. He opened the door and everyone went outside. But as they all walked toward the rover, Susannah suddenly turned.

"I forgot something," she said. "I'll be right back."

"Don't waste any time, Susannah," said Nelson. "We want to make some progress before it rains."

Susannah hurried back into the dome and into the

main work area. Her eyes darted from shelf to shelf. Then she spotted what she wanted. She grabbed it, stuck it into a pocket, and rushed back outside.

Nelson, Doc, and Brent were sitting in the rover with Nelson in the driver's seat. Susannah flung herself into the back, next to Brent. Then Nelson started the engine and they headed away from the dome. Susannah turned to wave to her mother and the others who were staying behind.

Meanwhile, Doc was unfolding a rough map that he had made. "As discussed," he said, "we'll head southwest. The churrs have always appeared from the west. And the ruined structures Brent saw are southwest of the dome. So we'll explore in that direction."

Nelson maneuvered the rover around rocks and through the valleys that separated the hills. It wasn't long before they were in territory none of them had seen before. It was more hilly here. And there was also a difference in the rocks that studded the tops of the hills. More of them were crystalline instead of dull blue. They glimmered in the harsh light of Openworld's sun.

Susannah slipped her goggles up on her forehead to see if the appearance of the rocks would change. No, they still looked like crystals. She put the goggles in place again.

Nelson glanced sideways toward Doc. "What if we find churrs and they don't seem friendly? What's our plan then?"

"If that happens, we retreat," said Doc. "We already know our tazers aren't much use against them. So getting away from them is the only thing to do if there's trouble."

"I still say they're not a threat," said Susannah stubbornly. "They helped us. I don't see any reason to expect that they'd want to hurt us." She paused. "Unless we hurt them," she added.

The group fell silent after that. Nelson concentrated on finding the smoothest possible route for the rover. The others studied the landscape intently. They were looking for any strange, glowing light that might indicate the presence of churrs. Or for signs of more broken-down buildings.

Nelson threaded the rover through a narrow valley, then drove along the base of a hill. Suddenly Brent shouted, "Stop!"

The rover lurched to a halt. "What is it?" asked Doc. "Do you see something?"

"Yes," replied Brent. He pointed to a spot about halfway up a gentle hill. "Look up there. I can see a glow."

The others gazed intently at the place indicated by Brent. "I see it!" cried Susannah. "It's faint, but I can see it."

"So can I," murmured Doc.

"Well, I can't," sputtered Nelson.

"Look again," suggested Susannah.

Nelson pushed his goggles up a bit further on his nose

and stared intently at the hill. "OK," he admitted. "I do see something."

"Well, let's investigate," said Doc. "But first, I'll check in with the folks at the dome so they know what we're doing."

Doc activated his communicator and had a quick conversation with Wally. He turned it off and said, "He warned us to be careful. I assured him we would be."

"I'll lead the way," offered Brent as they all climbed out of the rover. "I think I can see things a bit better than the rest of you."

They followed Brent slowly uphill. The closer they got, the more pronounced the glow became. Now they could see that the strange light outlined an arched opening.

"It's a doorway," said Brent as they approached the glowing arch. "Should we go in?"

Doc stepped back a few paces and studied the entrance. "It doesn't look like a natural cave opening," he said. "It looks like someone built it—cut it into the side of the hill." He moved forward and pushed against the sides of the arch. "Seems sturdy," he said thoughtfully. Then he turned to the rest of the group.

"I'm going to go in. If any of you want to wait outside, that's fine."

"I want to come, too!" exclaimed Susannah. The others echoed her.

Doc nodded. Then he stepped through the doorway

with three followers close on his heels. Both Doc and Nelson had to duck slightly to avoid hitting their heads.

They were in a wide tunnel. Light from outside reflected off the polished walls. "It's almost like glass," marveled Susannah.

"And definitely not natural," added Doc. "It would take a lot of effort to make rock this smooth."

As they continued, they began to go downhill. The light faded a bit. However, the reflected light was enough to let them see. Or perhaps it was because of the glow that they could pick up with their goggles.

Suddenly Doc stopped. "Listen!" he said in a whisper.

As the sound of their footsteps died, they could all hear it. A low churring sound. "They're in here," said Nelson. "We've found them!"

"Shhh!" commanded Doc. Then, moving even more slowly than before, he resumed walking.

Susannah noted that the level of the light increased as they moved forward. Ahead of them, the walls widened slightly and curved sharply to the right. Walking single file, the four explorers rounded the corner.

The tunnel suddenly opened into a large, high-ceilinged room. A cluster of churrs hovered in the middle of the space, as if waiting for them.

Susannah stared at them in wonder. The furry creatures no longer looked like gray blobs to her. Instead, they shimmered with a lovely, soft light.

"You never said how beautiful they look," she whispered to Brent.

"I guess I didn't think about them as beautiful," he whispered back.

They fell silent as the churrs began to move forward. Soon they were only two feet away.

No one moved—neither churr nor human. It was a standoff of sorts. Susannah wondered what they should do. Did they dare move forward, hoping the churrs would allow them to do so? Or should they go back up to the entrance and not risk angering the creatures?

Still, she felt no real sense of threat from the churrs. It was more a sense of waiting. Taking a deep breath, she let herself relax. Her eyes darted from left to right, studying her surroundings with interest.

Then she noticed something. Niches had been cut into the glassy rock walls. And in almost every niche stood a small object. A pale green stone, smoothed and carved into a pleasing shape. Susannah nudged Doc. With a dip of her head, she indicated the display.

Doc's eyes widened. "So the stone you found *does* belong to the churrs," he murmured.

Susannah nodded. Then she reached into her pocket. She pulled out the green stone she and Brent had found near the water hole. With her goggles on, it glowed with a strange and beautiful light. Almost as if she were looking at it through sun-licked water.

Doc looked from the stone to Susannah's face. In a low

voice, she answered his unspoken sentence. "I thought it was theirs. And that we should return it."

Nelson and Brent had been watching silently. Now Brent grinned and gave Susannah a thumbs-up signal.

She turned to face the hovering churrs. I wish I could talk to them, she thought. Then she took a deep breath. She took one step forward. The churrs didn't move.

Susannah opened her hand so the stone was visible. "This is yours," she said. "We brought it back to you."

At the sight of the stone, the churring sound grew louder. And the creatures' fur seemed to glow even brighter than it had before.

Susannah took another step. Then another. Slowly she walked toward an empty niche. She placed the sculpture there, then stepped back.

The churring became almost deafening. Then it ebbed. The cluster of creatures parted in the middle. They fanned out in two lines, forming what looked like an honor guard.

"I think they want us to keep going," Susannah said. Without hesitation, she started forward, walking between the two lines of churrs.

The creatures kept up a gentle humming. They hovered beside the four humans, as if guiding them on their journey.

At the other side of the room there was another tunnel. Several churrs slipped through its arched entry.

Susannah followed the churrs. It was darker inside this

tunnel than it had been in the first. However, the glow given off by the churrs provided enough light to see her way.

She turned once, to reassure herself that the others were with her. Then, somehow trusting the churrs, she forged ahead.

After a few moments, the tunnel began to fill with light. Susannah stepped through another arched entryway—and into a huge, marvelous world like nothing she had ever seen before. Her gasps of amazement were echoed by her fellow explorers.

Civilization

A stunning sight stood before the four humans. They were in a huge cavern—so large that they couldn't make out details at the other side. The entire area was bathed in light.

"Look," breathed Susannah in wonder. She pointed toward the roof of the cavern. A huge crystalline dome

seemed to float overhead. It somehow softened and gentled Pele's harsh rays.

From the floor of the cavern, towers of every size and shape rose into the air. Some were rounded, others needle-sharp. Arching bridges and curved ramps connected many of the towers. The light from above sparkled down in rainbows of color. The crystals acted as a prism, casting blue, green, and violet rays onto the polished surfaces of the structures below.

Between the towers, plants grew in carefully tended beds. Susannah saw each of the varieties she had seen on the surface of the planet. But there were others as well. And they all grew much taller and more lushly here. Especially

where there was water—for several sparkling streams were fed by small waterfalls that tumbled down the sides of the great chamber.

And wherever Susannah looked, she saw churrs. Thousands of churrs. The room hummed with their sound. They hovered near the towers and in the gardens. They sat upon the bridges and ramps. They were everywhere.

Again Susannah's gaze went to the top of the cavern. "Those crystals we saw at the top of some of the hills must all be roofs," she said. "But how do they stay up?"

"I think these structures are similar to geodesic domes," Doc explained. "It's kind of hard to explain—but basically they hold themselves up."

"Whoever built this knows something about architecture," Nelson added.

"The churrs created it," said Brent excitedly. "I'm sure of it! Look!"

Susannah looked where Brent was pointing. Several churrs hovered just above the floor of the chamber, near a great block of rough stone. As she watched, they surrounded the stone. Their glow became more pronounced and their fur quivered wildly. Then they moved away. The stone's surface now gleamed and reflected the light. And instead of a rectangular block, it was tapered. Just like the base of the tower that stood next to it.

"They shaped it!" cried Susannah. "But how?"

"I have no idea," replied Doc, his voice tinged with wonder. "They must be able to harness energy somehow. Or use thought waves. Or—who knows? Certainly it's beyond my comprehension."

"They obviously wanted us to see this," Susannah commented. "But I don't think they want us to go any further." She indicated the line of churrs that hovered between them and the main part of the cavern. "So what should we do now?"

"Do?" repeated Nelson. "We have to report this back to Earth. This is an astounding discovery! An actual civilization on another planet."

Susannah stared at Nelson in dismay. "If we do that, everyone will want to come here to study the churrs."

"Yes, of course," said Nelson.

"That would be awful!"

"All right, we're not going to argue about it here," said Doc. He looked out at the rainbow city. Then at the churrs that lingered nearby. "I think we should leave now. We have to get in touch with the dome, anyway. And I don't want to risk using a communicator here."

Susannah studied the scene before her as if trying to memorize it. It's amazing, she thought. Beautiful—and amazing. Then she turned and followed Doc and the others back through the tunnel. A group of churrs escorted them all the way to the surface. There, the creatures hovered in the doorway.

Susannah looked at them. "Good-bye," she whispered. And then she made a silent promise. I'll try to protect you, she thought. I'll try not to let this be destroyed.

"Come on, Susannah," called Nelson. "We have to get back to the dome."

She trudged downhill toward the rover.

Two hours later they were back at the dome. Angie, Laura, and Wally had been waiting anxiously. Now they listened in stunned silence to the story the four explorers had to tell.

When they had finished, Laura looked at her daughter. "What made you take the stone with you?" she asked.

Susannah shrugged. "It was just a feeling I had," she admitted. She looked at Doc. "I should have asked you, I suppose."

Doc smiled. "Your instincts are good, Susannah. I'm glad you trusted them. I think giving the stone back made the churrs feel less threatened by us. I think that's why they let us see their city."

"So are you going to contact Earth about this, Doc?" asked Nelson. "Or do you want me to make a report?"

"What would you say?" asked Susannah.

"Why, I'd tell everyone we've found a marvelous site to

colonize," Nelson replied. "Think about it. We can build inside the hills, just like the churrs have."

"We can't!" protested Susannah.

"What do you mean?"

"Yes, Susannah, what do you mean?" asked Doc.

Susannah looked at the six faces before her. She had to make them understand. She had to! She took a deep breath and started talking.

"Yes, it's a wonderful planet," she began. "But is it for humans?" She looked at Brent, pleading for his support. "You saw what happened on the surface," she said. "Where we had walked, things were smashed and ruined."

"I thought it was all ruined anyway," said Wally.

"Well, yes, but Susannah's right," Brent added. "We had done even more damage."

"So think of what having humans here might do to the churrs' underground civilization," Susannah said. "Even with special goggles, we might not be able to see everything. It's clear that something destroyed their original civilization on the surface of the planet. Do we want to destroy what they have now?"

"There's no proof that it was *their* civilization on the surface," said Nelson.

"Actually, I think you're wrong, Nelson," observed Brent. "I've seen the ruined towers. They are almost identical to the ones we saw in the cavern."

"Still," protested Wally, "these churrs have a lot to offer

science. We can study them to find out how they channel energy. How they're able to build without arms or hands or tools of any sort."

"You mean study them like lab rats?" asked Susannah. "Put them in cages? Experiment with them?"

"Well . . . When you make an omelette, a few eggs have to get broken," said Wally.

"I think we humans have broken a few too many eggs," Susannah observed in a soft voice. "All through history that's what we've done. To all kinds of civilizations."

She continued, looking from face to face as she made her plea. "The churrs—or some other creature—once had a civilization on the surface of this planet. Something happened to destroy it. A change in climate, maybe. Or some natural disaster. Or maybe it was visitors from another planet.

"Whatever happened, the churrs have still managed to create a wonderful world for themselves. A world that humans would enjoy sharing. But think about this: What are the chances that our colonization will ruin what they have? Or at least change it drastically?"

Here she paused and looked directly at Doc. "What are the chances?" she asked again.

Doc shook his head. "To be honest—about 99%, Susannah. There is no question that colonization will mean change for the churrs."

Having said that, Doc rose to his feet. "We have some

important decisions to make. Let's all get a good night's sleep. Tomorrow we'll talk about what to do next."

Let it be the right decision, Susannah thought.

15

Decisions

Susannah tossed and turned all night. And, from the appearance of her fellow colonists the next morning, she wasn't the only one.

"Well," Doc said, "let's talk about what we're going to do."

"I vote for not telling anyone about the churrs," Susannah said immediately.

"Me, too," added Brent.

"Just a minute," Wally said. He looked at Susannah and Brent. "I understand how you feel. But there's something we didn't talk about yesterday."

"I was wondering who would bring that up," said Doc. "At least, I think I know what you're going to say."

Wally nodded. "You probably do, Doc." Then he went on. "OK, suppose we all agree that the churrs should be left alone. That means *we* need to leave Openworld. That *no* humans should live here."

"I *did* think about that," said Susannah slowly. "And I *don't* think we should stay."

Angie sighed loudly. "So you're saying we should just

move on. After all the work we've done here already. Even though it looks like this planet would be a perfect place to colonize."

"It would be perfect if the churrs didn't already live here," Susannah pointed out. "But they do."

Laura spoke up. "I know this is a hard decision for all of us. However, I also think we should move on. There are other planets in this solar system that may be habitable. Perhaps we can find one that doesn't already have a civilization."

"Perhaps we can't and have to return to Earth," said Wally.

"That's a chance we have to take," commented Laura.

Wally shook his head. "Look, I basically agree with you guys. But we're scientists. We've made a major discovery. Do we have the right to keep it from the rest of the world?"

Angie made her contribution to the discussion. "I think we *do* have that right, Wally. I think it's up to us to decide what makes a planet habitable. And I think most of us feel that a place with creatures that humans could harm is not a place where we should settle."

"Someone else may come along later."

"Maybe. But then it will be their decision what to do. Not ours."

Wally threw his hands into the air. "OK, OK! I admit it. I don't want to be responsible for ruining the churrs' world. So I say we go."

Doc turned to Nelson. "It sounds like most of us feel the same way, Nelson. However, I'm not sure you agree. I'd like to hear your thoughts. We all would."

There was a long silence. Then Nelson got to his feet. "I was awake most of the night," he said, "thinking about what we saw. And about what Susannah said."

Susannah was startled at that admission. She hadn't thought Nelson had listened to her at all.

"Doc, we're all scientists. Even Brent and Susannah are—far more than most kids their ages. And as scientists, we want to make discoveries. To learn new things. That's our job. That's why we all signed on for this mission."

He smiled and looked directly at Susannah. "However, Susannah is more than a budding scientist. She's also our historian. And she's reminded us that humans have made some serious mistakes in the past."

Now it was as if he was speaking to himself. "You know, when physicians finish their training, they take an oath. They make a promise. And part of that promise is to do no harm. That's what kept going through my head last night: do no harm."

"Are you saying—"

Nelson interrupted Susannah's question. "I'm saying I agree with you. I don't think we should tell anyone what we found here. And I do think we should look for another planet to colonize."

At first Susannah was too stunned to move. But then

she got up and walked over to Nelson. "Thank you," she murmured.

"Thank *you*," said Nelson.

"It's unanimous, then," announced Doc. "And that means we have a lot to do."

That afternoon, Doc radioed to Earth. He explained that the communications problem had been cleared up. That a decision had been made to move on to another planet. That Openworld was not ideal for colonization.

The next week passed quickly. Wally checked the *Leif* from top to bottom to be sure it was ready to travel. Laura and Susannah packed seeds and plant samples. Perhaps they would grow on the next planet they reached.

Everyone worked on dismantling the dome and making the *Leif's* parachute operational for another landing.

At last it was time to leave Openworld. Susannah stood at one of the spacecraft's viewing ports, looking at the blue landscape outside. Her mother stood beside her.

"I wonder what's next for us?" Susannah asked.

"An adventure, I'm sure," said Laura. She put an arm around her daughter's shoulders. "Whatever it is, we'll face it together. All of us."

"Into your seats, everyone!" called Wally. "It's time."

Susannah strapped herself into her seat. A moment later, Wally started the *Leif's* engines. There was a roar as the thrusters pulsed. The ship shuddered.

As the *Leif* rose from the blue surface of Openworld, Susannah thought about the trip ahead. The force of their rockets would take the ship back to the lightsail where it orbited the planet. Once the *Leif* was reconnected to the sail, Pele's light would power the ship away from the pull of Openworld's gravity. And then on to another planet.

Suddenly an image filled her mind. One she had read about and thought about many times before. It was an image of a ship. But not the *Leif*. It was a different kind of ship, with a different kind of sail. An ocean-going vessel navigated by explorers with dreams of conquest. A vessel headed for distant shores where civilizations already existed.

And on those shores, people stood and stared at the white sails. Their minds were filled with curiosity—and their hearts with an unexplainable dread.

But this time, the image changed for Susannah. This time, something unusual happened.

The ship turned around and sailed away.